*Quito shut the door to the sleek, black sports car and stepped back. "Will I see you again before you leave?"*

It wouldn't be wise. The few minutes she'd spent with him already were burned into her memory. "I don't know. Do you want to?"

A devilish smile suddenly crooked his mouth and he bent his head through the open window and kissed her. For a moment she was stunned and then, slowly, her mouth opened and her hand came up to cup the side of his face.

How could it be that the taste of him, the feel of his lips, were so sweetly the same? she wondered. And how could it be that she still wanted him so badly?

By the time he pulled his head back from hers, she could feel her pulse beating wildly in her temples.

"What do you think?" he asked.

Dear Reader,

Well, as promised, the dog days of summer have set in, which means one last chance at the beach reading that's an integral part of this season (even if you do most of it on the subway, like I do!). We begin with *The Beauty Queen's Makeover* by Teresa Southwick, next up in our MOST LIKELY TO... miniseries. She was the girl "most likely to" way back when, and he was the awkward geek. Now they've all but switched places, and the fireworks are about to begin....

In *From Here to Texas*, Stella Bagwell's next MEN OF THE WEST book, a Navajo man and the girl who walked out on him years ago have to decide if they believe in second chances. And speaking of second chances (or first ones, anyway), picture this: a teenaged girl obsessed with a gorgeous college boy writes down some of her impure thoughts in her diary, and buries said diary in the walls of an old house in town. Flash forward ten-ish years, and the boy, now a man, is back in town—and about to dismantle the old house, brick by brick. Can she find her diary before he does? Find out in Christine Flynn's finale to her GOING HOME miniseries, *Confessions of a Small-Town Girl*. In *Everything She's Ever Wanted* by Mary J. Forbes, a traumatized woman is finally convinced to come out of hiding, thanks to the one man she can trust. In Nicole Foster's *Sawyer's Special Delivery*, a man who's played knight-in-shining armor gets to do it again—to a woman (cum newborn baby) desperate for his help, even if she hates to admit it. And in *The Last Time I Saw Venice* by Vivienne Wallington, a couple traumatized by the loss of their child hopes that the beautiful city that brought them together can work its magic—one more time.

So have your fun. And next month it's time to get serious—about reading, that is....

Enjoy!

Gail Chasan
Senior Editor

Please address questions and book requests to:
Silhouette Reader Service
U.S.: 3010 Walden Ave., P.O. Box 1325, Buffalo, NY 14269
Canadian: P.O. Box 609, Fort Erie, Ont. L2A 5X3

# FROM HERE TO TEXAS

*Stella Bagwell*

**SPECIAL EDITION**

Published by Silhouette Books

**America's Publisher of Contemporary Romance**

To my editor, Stacy Boyd, for being such a dear joy to
work with. Thank you for keeping me on the right track.

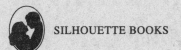 **SILHOUETTE BOOKS**

ISBN 0-373-24700-1

FROM HERE TO TEXAS

Copyright © 2005 by Stella Bagwell

This edition published by arrangement with Harlequin Books S.A.

Visit Silhouette Books at www.eHarlequin.com

**Printed in U.S.A.**

## STELLA BAGWELL

sold her first book to Silhouette in November 1985. More than fifty novels later, she still loves her job and says she isn't completely content unless she's writing. Recently she and her husband moved from the hills of Oklahoma to Seadrift, Texas, a sleepy little fishing town located on the coastal bend. Stella says the water, the tropical climate and the seabirds make it a lovely place to let her imagination soar and to put the stories in her head down on paper.

She and her husband have one son, Jason, who lives and teaches high school math in nearby Port Lavaca.

My darling Clementine,

Morning is dawning and as I watch the sun rise over the desert mountains, I can hardly wait for the day to come and the hours to pass before I can be with you again.

The scent of you, the taste of you, the feel of your soft body next to mine runs deep in my blood and I realize I am a lost man.

I understand that we come from different worlds and that you're afraid to try to live in mine. But when we make love I believe we both forget that I am Mexican and Navajo and that you are from a rich, white family.

If you go back to Texas, my love, my broken heart will go with you for always.

Love,

Quito

# Chapter One

Quito Perez was sweating by the time he walked into the Wagon Wheel Café and, though he hated sitting close to the door, he sank onto the first available bar stool rather than work his way toward a booth in the back.

Damn it! He hated the weak quiver in his legs, the labored breathing after two blocks of simple walking. Even so, he was grateful to God to still be alive.

A month had passed since someone had driven up beside his SUV and blasted three nine millimeter slugs at him. The bullets had smashed into his vehicle and gone on to shatter his ribs, collapse a lung and rip his spleen to shreds. But he'd cheated the murdering bastard who'd tried to kill him. He'd survived.

"Hey, Sheriff, how's it going today?"

He looked up to see Betty, a middle-aged waitress who'd worked at the Wagon Wheel for as long as he could remember. She had coarse features and rough hands but she was a hardworking woman with a soft heart. He could always count on her for good service and a sympathetic word.

"I can't complain, Betty. I saw the sunrise this morning."

With an understanding smile, she reached across the countertop and patted his hand. "We all prayed for you, Sheriff, while you were down. And see, you're already up and around and back in the saddle," she said brightly.

Quito wasn't exactly back in the saddle completely. But a week ago, he'd finally returned to light duty at his desk. It was great to be back at work, yet he wished he could go at full throttle. He was a man who'd never been sick or down with an injury. Having to coddle himself was a pain in the rear. One that he was more than ready to be rid of.

"I hope all the people around the county know how much I appreciate their thoughts and prayers," Quito told her. "I just wish I was back to full strength. Jess and Daniel are working themselves to death."

Betty pulled a pad and pen from a pocket on her

pink uniform. "I wouldn't worry one minute about those two lawmen of yours. They're young and in their prime. You can't work those two guys down. Besides, you'll be your old self before you know it. You just need some of Nadine's biscuits and eggs to put some tallow back on you."

"Add some bacon and hash browns to that and I'll eat it," he told her.

"I hear you," she said with a wide grin. The woman scribbled the order down on her pad, then hurried away to pour the sheriff a cup of coffee.

To his left and a few feet behind him, Quito heard the cowbell jingle as the door to the café opened and closed. Seconds later, a strong male hand was squeezing his shoulder.

"Mornin' Quito."

He didn't have to look up to know the greeting had come from his under sheriff, Jess Hastings. The tall, sandy-haired lawman had been his right-hand man for nearly three years now. Between Jess and their chief deputy, Daniel Redwing, he hadn't had to worry about law and order being kept in the county while he recuperated. The two men could be trusted completely.

"Good morning, Jess. Where's Redwing? Isn't he going to eat breakfast with us this morning?"

Jess grinned slyly as he slung a leg over the adjacent bar stool. "Maggie is seeing that Daniel gets fed."

The deputy had married Jess's widowed sister-in-law three weeks ago. Quito had barely been released from the hospital and had still been wearing drain tubes at the time, but he'd managed to sit on the church pew long enough to see the pair exchange their wedding vows. The wedding had been one of the happier moments he'd had since he'd been shot.

Quito chuckled. "Oh, yeah, sometimes I forget he's a newlywed."

"Well, it was quite a shock to see the guy walk down the aisle. I thought he hated women." Jess grunted with amusement. "Little did I know."

Betty reappeared with Quito's coffee along with another cup for Jess. She took Jesse's order and hurried away to a customer who was motioning for her attention.

Quito took a sip of the sustaining caffeine then glanced over at his friend and fellow lawman. "Don't suppose you've had any new leads come into your desk. Leads about the shooting, that is," he added, even though he figured Jess understood.

The other man glumly shook his head. "Not anything credible. We've had all sorts of people saying they saw a black Dodge with heavily tinted windows in the area the day you were shot, but no one has any idea of the tag number. One guy thinks it had Nevada plates, but hell, the thing could have been rented."

Quito shook his head. "I doubt it, Jess. Pickup

trucks aren't big rental vehicles. A person wouldn't need a truck, he could shoot out of a car just as easily."

Jess shrugged. "Yeah, but in a truck the shooter would be sitting up higher and have a better view at the target."

Quito resisted shuddering at the fact that he'd been the target. "That's true." He took another sip of the coffee and rubbed the palm of his hand against his brow. It came away wet even though the room was air-conditioned. "You know, Jess, I lay awake at night—wondering who the hell hates me enough to want me dead. I can't think of anyone. Or maybe I just don't want to think any of my friends isn't really a friend."

Jess shook his head. "Listen, Quito, I know what you're thinking—what you're going through. It doesn't do any good to let yourself start getting paranoid about everyone around you."

More than a year ago, Jess had also been shot while investigating a murder. The bullet had knocked him over into a deep ravine and the fall itself had nearly killed him, not to mention all the blood that he'd lost. Thankfully they'd eventually found the shooter and a jury had sentenced him to many long years in the penitentiary.

"You're right," Quito replied. "I just need to keep my eyes and ears open. That's all."

"And you need to get completely well before you

start working ten to twelve hours a day," Jess told him. "Bet the doctor has already given you those orders."

Quito nodded. "Don't worry, Jess, I'm taking things slow. Well, as slow as I can."

From the other end of the busy diner, Betty appeared through a set of swinging doors. She was carrying a tray loaded with two platters of breakfast food and she headed straight for the two San Juan County lawmen.

"Here you go, guys." She placed the steaming food in front of them. "I'll get you some more coffee. Want anything else?"

The two men both assured her they were content and they dug into their eggs and biscuits. As they ate, they continued to talk about the few leads they'd had on Quito's shooting before they finally turned their attention to a recent rash of burglaries.

Jess had just finished the last bite on his plate when his pager went off. After he checked the message, he told Quito he had to go and threw down a bill large enough to pay for several meals.

"Hey, this is too much money!" Quito called after him.

Jess waved a hand as he hurried out the door. "You can buy next time."

He gave the bill to Betty and she went to the cash register to pay both men out. While he waited for her to return with the change, he sipped the last of his coffee and glanced around the long room. It was seven-thirty and the place was jammed with customers. A nonsmoking policy had never been enforced in the eating place and the blue-gray clouds waved and dipped through the air as diners ate and read the *Farmington Daily*.

Betty got caught at the register and ended up waiting on several customers before she finally returned with Quito's change. As she counted the change out to him, she said with a wide grin, "Looks like Jess was feeling generous this morning. Guess that's what living with Victoria does to the man. When are you ever going to find yourself a good woman, Quito?"

Just as he started to tell her there weren't any good women who'd put up with him, the cowbell jangled and Betty eyed the potential customer with great interest.

"Uh—maybe that's her right there," she murmured under her breath.

Quito slowly looked over his shoulder and immediately felt as though someone had smashed him in the gut.

Dear God, it was Clementine Jones!

Without even glancing his way, she walked past him and eased into an empty booth. For a moment, as Quito watched her settle herself on the vinyl seat, he thought his lung must have collapsed again. He couldn't breathe in or out and his heart was racing, tripping weakly against his busted ribs.

"Sheriff? Is that someone you know?"

The question had come from Betty and he looked around to see the waitress was still standing across the counter from him. Her curious gaze was wavering between him and Clementine.

"Yeah," he said grimly. "I thought I knew her." He adjusted the brim of his gray Stetson and slid from the bar stool. "Excuse me, Betty. Oh, here you go." He tossed an extra nice tip on the table and walked away from the bar.

Clementine didn't notice his approach. She was too busy folding away her designer sunglasses and stowing them in a leather handbag.

Once he was standing at the side of her table, he said in a low voice, "Hello, Clementine."

The greeting caused her head to jerk up. Recognition flashed in her eyes and just as quickly her rosy-beige skin turned the color of a sick olive.

"Hello, Quito."

His nostrils flared as he tried to draw in the oxygen his body was craving. Clementine Jones was as beautiful, no he mentally corrected himself, she was even more beautiful than he remembered. Her waist-length hair was straight and glossy and the color of a west Texas wheat field just before harvest time. Eyes as blue as a New Mexican sky were almond shaped and fringed with long dark lashes. Her lips were full and bow shaped, and at the moment naked. The point of her chin was slightly dented and though it wasn't evident now, when she smiled there was a dimple in her left cheek.

Clementine looked as classy and out of place in this diner, Quito thought, as a Mustang would in Linc Ketchum's remuda on the T Bar K.

"This is quite a surprise," he said, "seeing you back in town."

Her gaze fluttered awkwardly away from his as she shrugged a long strand of hair back over her shoulder. "Yes, it's been a while."

"Eleven years is a long time," he stated.

The idea that he'd kept count had her gaze swinging back to his. Pink color seeped into the skin covering her high, slanted cheekbones.

"How have you been, Quito? Still the sheriff, I see."

Something inside him snapped, then ricocheted around in him as her gaze slipped to the badge pinned to the left side of his chest.

"I'm making it, okay. The people around here still want me as their peacemaker and I'm glad to oblige."

His drawl held the faintest edge and she must have picked up on the sharpness because the corners of her lips tightened ever so slightly.

"Must be nice to be wanted," she murmured.

"You ought to know," he countered softly. "See ya' around, Clem."

He turned away from the booth to leave and noticed Betty heading toward them with her pad and pencil.

As he started toward the exit Quito jerked his thumb back at Clementine's booth. "Treat her right, Betty. She's used to the best."

Clementine tried not to look at the man as he left the café, but her eyes seemed to have a mind of their own and she watched his tall, solidly built body ease past the glass door and out of sight.

"Good mornin', miss. You havin' breakfast this mornin'?"

Sighing with a sadness she dared not examine, Clementine turned back to the waitress hovering at the edge of her table.

"Just coffee and toast. And maybe a little jam— any kind will do," she told the waitress.

Betty quickly scribbled the order down then cast a faint grin at Clementine. "You must be new around town. I'd remember someone as pretty as you."

Clementine flushed at Betty's compliment. "Thank you. I used to live in this area for a while. I'm just back for a short visit."

Curiosity raised Betty's eyebrows. "Oh. You lived here in town? I live on Fourth. Little yellow house with a mesquite tree in the front yard."

Clementine shook her head as she told herself she was going to have to get used to this. People were naturally going to be asking her why she was here, how long she planned to stay and where she'd been. The best thing she could do was to be honest.

"I didn't live here in town. My parents owned the house south of town—the white stucco with the red tile roof. It's on the mountain."

Since there was only one house that fit that description, Betty's mouth formed a silent *O*. "You mean the Jones house?"

Clementine nodded. "I didn't know if anyone would remember. It's been a long time since we were here."

Betty was flat out amazed. "Remember? Why, honey, everyone remembers you Joneses."

"Hey, Betty! Are you gonna talk all day over there or are you gonna pour me some coffee?"

The waitress glanced over at the man sitting on a bar stool. Even though his griping appeared to be good-natured, she stuck her pencil behind her ear and said, "Gotta go, miss. I'll bring that toast right out."

After Clementine ate breakfast she drove down main street and parked her black sports car in front of a log structure with a sign hanging over the door that read Neil Rankin, Attorney at Law.

Small sprinklers were dampening the patches of grass in front of the building. To the right-hand side of the steps stood a huge blue spruce tree. The pungent scent from its boughs was fresh and crisp to Clementine's nostrils and she could only think how different this little corner of the world was from Houston and many of the poverty-stricken places she'd visited in the past couple of years. The sky was clean and sharply blue. The scents of evergreen, juniper and sage laced the dry air. And the men were just as rough and tough as any Texan on the streets of Houston. Especially one, she thought. The one with a badge on his shirt and a gun on his hips.

Feeling as though every last bit of air had drained from her lungs, she slumped back against the seat and passed a trembling hand across her forehead.

*Why are you so upset, Clementine? You knew you were going to run into the man sometime during this stay. You knew you were going to have to look upon his face again.*

Drawing in a ragged breath, she tried to push the voice away and gather her shaken senses.

She turned her gaze on the passenger window and stared out at the town where she'd once walked and shopped. Above the roofs of the buildings, in the far, far distance, the peaks of the San Juan Mountains were capped with snow and as she studied their majestic beauty, her thoughts turned backward to a time when she and Quito had walked along a quiet mountain path. Even though it had been summer, patches of snow had lain in the shadows and in the meadows dandelions as big as saucers had bobbed in the warm sun. She and Quito had lain down in the grass and the wildflowers and made love. The trees and the sky had been their canopy and the earth had been their bed. She'd fallen in love with him that day and her life had never been the same since.

Several minutes passed before Clementine was composed enough to leave the car and enter the lawyer's office. The front area of the building was modestly decorated with plastic chairs and a coffee table loaded with magazines. In the center of the room, close to a door marked Private, was a wide desk with an Hispanic woman seated behind it. A nameplate on the corner said her name was Connie Jimenez.

As Clementine approached the desk, the woman continued to chat on the telephone. After two long minutes, she hung up and quickly apologized.

"Sorry about that. Some people think they can butt their way into anything." The middle-aged woman had black, slightly graying hair and she smiled at Clementine with a sincerity that was real, not like the phony lip movement she saw back in the city. "What can I do for you?"

"I'm Clementine Jones. Neil told me to drop by this morning. Is he busy?"

Connie rolled her eyes as if to say Neil Rankin wouldn't know what real work was. "He's probably in there throwing darts."

Clementine's brows arched upward. "Why? Is he angry?"

Connie laughed. "Angry? Are you kidding? I've never seen that man even raise his voice. He's practicing his dart game for a tournament down at Indian Wells. That's a local bar and grill. First prize gets you free beer for a year."

She motioned toward the door marked Private. "Go on in. I just made him a fresh pot of coffee. And there're doughnuts, too."

"Thanks," Clementine told her and knocked lightly before she opened the door to Neil Rankin's office.

As Connie had predicted, the lawyer was drinking coffee and throwing darts at a board on the wall.

"Come in," he called as he walked over to the dart board and plucked one from the center of the target. "I'll be right with you."

"It's only me, Neil."

The sound of her voice caused him to jerk with surprise and he quickly turned and hurried over. The smile on his face said he was truly glad to see her and she was relieved. It was no secret that the relationship between Neil and Quito had been a long, close one. She couldn't blame Neil if he hated her for hurting his friend.

"Clementine! How great to see you!"

Neil was a tall man with a handsomely chiseled face. Compared to Quito's rugged build, he was slender, but well put together and his dark blond hair was naturally streaked and fell across his forehead in a boyish fashion. He'd been single when she'd been living here and from the looks of his empty ring finger he was still that way. It was hard to believe some woman hadn't snared him before now, she thought. But then, maybe he'd been burned as she'd been burned. Maybe he never wanted to think about the word *love*.

He took both her hands and gave them a warm squeeze. Clementine couldn't help but smile at him. "Hello, Neil."

Neil positioned a cushioned chair in front of his desk and helped her into it. "I was just drinking my morning coffee. Let me get you a cup," he said.

She'd already had two cups at the Wagon Wheel, but now that she was here she wanted to appear sociable. "That would be nice. Thank you," she told him.

He walked over to the coffeemaker and picked up a glass cup. "I'll give you good china," he said with a wink. "Connie says I shouldn't give a lady a cup of coffee in a foam cup. Cream or sugar?"

"Cream please."

The lawyer carried it over to her and she smiled wryly as she accepted the cup and saucer. "At least you think I'm a lady," she said.

Frowning, he rested his hips on the front of the desk. "Now why would you say that? I've always considered you a lady."

A blush crept across her face. "Well, I don't imagine you've had too many good thoughts of me since I left Aztec. You and Quito were such good friends."

He shrugged. "And we still are. I don't put the entire blame on your breakup with you. You were very young then, Clementine. Quito should have realized that and—well, let's not get into all that. Tell me what you're doing with the house?"

Neil walked around the desk and eased down in a leather chair. Clementine sipped her coffee and tried to get comfortable. "I don't know. That's why I wanted to talk to you about it first. I knew you'd be honest with me. As to whether I should sell or rent."

Thoughtful, he rubbed a thumb and forefinger across his dented chin. "The place has been empty for a long time. Years, in fact. Why have you suddenly decided to do something with it?"

Clementine breathed deeply. "Believe me, Neil, my decision isn't sudden. I've had the place on my mind for a long while. But I—" She couldn't continue. She couldn't admit to this old friend that she'd been afraid to return to Aztec, afraid of facing Quito and all that had happened between them. "I've been busy with one thing and another," she finished.

He smiled understandingly. "Well, the years have certainly been kind to you, Clementine. You haven't aged a day. You're still just as pretty as ever."

"And it sounds like you're still the flirt and flatterer that I remember," she teased.

Neil chuckled and then his expression turned serious. "I thought that you might have come back because of Quito. You must have heard he nearly died."

The news was such a slam to her stomach she actually pressed her hand against her midsection. Incredulous, she stared at him. "Nearly died? But how? Why?"

"Someone tried to murder him. It happened out on highway 544. Someone drove up beside him and pumped three nine millimeter slugs into the side of his vehicle. Two of the bullets hit Quito and did a lot of damage. He only got released from the hospital about two or three weeks ago."

So that's why he'd looked a little pale, she thought. And all the time he'd been standing beside her table, she'd been thinking his ashen color had been a result of seeing her again. Clementine should have known better than to think she'd had that much effect on the man.

Still stunned, she slowly shook her head. "No—I—I hadn't heard about Quito. In fact, I just saw him over at the Wagon Wheel. He stopped by my table to say hello." A pained expression crossed her face. "He didn't say anything about being shot!"

Neil shrugged. "No. Quito wouldn't say anything. He's not the sort to go around talking about himself."

Or to her, she thought, sadly.

"I noticed he was still wearing his badge and gun.

So apparently he's not giving up the job of sheriff," she said to Neil.

Leaning back in his chair, Neil folded his arms across his chest and thoughtfully eyed her troubled face. "Why, Clementine, you sound as if you still care about our brave sheriff."

Trying to keep any sort of emotion from her face, Clementine reached down and pulled a set of thick papers from the briefcase she'd carried in with her handbag.

"Here's the abstract and deed for the house and land," she said stiffly. "Once you have a chance to read it over you can contact me at the Apache Junction."

Clementine rose to her feet and walked out before the lawyer collected himself enough to make any sort of reply.

Once she was outside and sitting in her car, she finally let her guard down. With a heavy sigh, she rested her forehead on the steering wheel and closed her eyes.

*Clementine, you sound as if you still care about our brave sheriff.*

What made Neil think she still had feelings for Quito Perez, she wondered bitterly. Eleven years was a long time. Love didn't last that long. Not for anybody.

## Chapter Two

After Clementine drove away from Neil Rankin's office, she decided at the last moment to turn the car onto the highway and drive out to the Jones house.

She'd only arrived in Aztec last night after a long drive up from Houston. Her mother, Delta, had pronounced her crazy for wanting to drive eleven hundred miles rather than fly to northern New Mexico. But Clementine hadn't wanted the trip to be short. She'd wanted the extra time to think about the past and ponder her future.

Nothing had turned out as she'd once planned and a tiny part of her hoped and believed that making this trip, and doing away with the house her parents had willed her, would finally put an end to her restless heart.

The car topped out on a small grade and Clementine automatically began to brake as she noticed a patrol car parked on the side of the road. It would be just her luck to get a speeding ticket, she thought dourly. Quito would surely get a laugh out of that.

On closer inspection, she noticed the car was empty and just as she was about to pass, she caught sight of a man's figure standing out among a stand of twisted juniper trees.

It was Quito!

Without bothering to wonder why, she steered her car onto the shoulder of the highway and parked in front of the patrol car. In a matter of seconds she was out of the car and walking toward him.

He noticed her immediately, but he didn't bother walking to meet her. Instead he stood his ground and waited for her to come to him.

She was still dressed in the slim white skirt and peach silk blouse she'd been wearing at the Wagon Wheel. The four-inch spiked heels on her feet were sinking into the loamy red soil and he cursed under his breath as she awkwardly covered the rough ground between them.

"What are you doing out here, Clementine?"

She licked her lips and smoothed her skirt. "I saw the car and then I spotted you. I thought something might be wrong." She hadn't exactly thought he was having trouble, but it was the only excuse she could think of at the moment. Apparently from the dry expression on Quito's face, he considered it pretty lame, too.

"Well, there's nothing wrong. And you're going to kill yourself wearing those heels out here like this."

A smile tilted the corners of her lips. "Still the ever practical Quito, I see."

Her blue eyes slid covertly down his six-foot-three-inch body. He was thick with muscle, much more so than he'd been eleven years ago. His thighs had his jeans stretched tight and the expanse across his chest and shoulders seemed to go on forever. He was wearing a white oxford shirt and the color contrasted starkly against his dark skin.

As her eyes returned to his face, she felt another kick in the stomach. Quito wasn't handsome. His features were far too rough for that. But the chiseled nose and mouth and dark hooded eyes all combined to make the most masculine face she'd ever seen. And one that, for her, had been unforgettable.

"I could think of worse things to be called," he said.

She smiled again while inside she sighed softly at the thought of stepping forward and laying her cheek against his broad chest. Quito was the strongest, bravest man she'd ever known. No one had ever made her feel as safe as he had.

"This morning—you didn't ask me why I was here in Aztec," she said. "How come?"

Her question sounded so much like the young nineteen-year-old woman he'd fallen in love with that he couldn't stop the corner of his lip from curling upward.

"Because it's none of my business why you're here."

She looked disappointed. Which didn't make an iota of sense to Quito. The woman had walked out of his life years ago. Granted, she'd said she was doing it all in the name of love. But she'd never come back to his little corner of the world. And for Quito that had pretty much exposed the truth of her feelings.

"Oh," she said and then a frown marred her pretty face. "Well, why didn't you tell me you'd been shot?"

So she'd heard about that already, he thought grimly. But hell, what did that matter, he reasoned. He wasn't trying to be a superhero in her eyes anymore.

"Look, Clementine, I just stopped by your table to say hello. That's all. What in hell do you expect from me, anyway?"

Her eyes were suddenly stricken with dark shadows and he couldn't miss the slight quiver of her lips as she murmured huskily, "I don't know, Quito."

Damn it, he was going to have to tell the doctor that something inside his chest had ripped open. Some of that sewing they'd done on him must have pulled apart because there was a pain between his lungs like he'd never felt before.

A hot westerly breeze picked up her long hair and she caught the shiny strands with her hand as she turned and walked away from him.

Torn with all sorts of emotions, Quito watched her for a few seconds, then cursed under his breath and hurried to catch up with her.

By the time his hand closed around her upper arm, his breathing was rapid and labored. Clementine stopped her forward motion and turned to study him with concern.

"Quito, are you all right?"

No, he was far from all right, he wanted to tell her. He'd had enough trouble this past month without the only woman he'd ever loved showing up to bring back all sorts of pain and misery.

"One of my lungs collapsed and two of my ribs were shattered from the gunfire. I'm not totally well yet," he admitted.

"I'm so sorry."

She looked both sincere and concerned but Quito wasn't going to be sucker enough to believe her this time.

"Yeah, I'm sorry, too," he muttered.

She drew in a long, bracing breath as she continued to hold her blond hair away from her face. "Look, Quito, for what it's worth I didn't come up here to cause you any sort of problems. My parents willed the house to me and I've come up to see about putting it on the market. That's all."

He forced the tension in his body to relax and only then did he realize his fingers were still gripping her upper arm. He dropped his hand and said, "I didn't really think you were here because of me. All of that was a long time ago. No sense in rehashing it."

Except that loving her still continued to affect his life. All the days and months and years that had spanned between them should have erased her from his mind, he thought helplessly. Yet the time hadn't done anything to dull the light of joy she brought to his heart.

She gave him a shaky smile. "I'm glad you feel that way, Quito." She glanced thoughtfully toward her car, then back at him. "I'm on my way to the house. Why don't you come with me? I haven't been there in years and I'm almost afraid of what I'll find."

His initial instinct was to turn down her invitation. He didn't need to spend any more time with this woman than necessary. But the hungry, wounded part of him couldn't resist. For years he'd dreamed about seeing this woman again. Now that she was here, he might as well live the dream a little longer, he thought.

"Sure. I haven't seen it in a long time, either," he said. "I'll follow you in the squad car."

With a nervous smile, she nodded. "See you there."

Had she gone crazy? Clementine asked herself as she started the car with shaky fingers and pulled onto the highway. What had possessed her to invite Quito to join her at the house?

*Silly woman you know why you invited him. Because you never could resist him and these next few minutes might be the last you ever have with him.*

Trying to put that black thought from her mind, Clementine concentrated on her driving and dared not to look in the rearview mirror. Just knowing he was directly behind her was enough to distract her.

Two miles passed before Clementine made a right-hand turn and pulled up to massive iron gates supported by two tall columns made of Colorado rock.

The gates were secured with a combination lock. She rolled the correct numbers and once the lock released she pushed the gates aside.

Before she slid back into her car, she walked back to the driver's window on Quito's car. He lowered the glass and looked at her.

"I just wanted to tell you not to bother locking the gates behind you. I've decided to leave them open while I'm here."

"All right," he replied.

She glanced toward the entrance. Clumps of sage had grown up around the rock columns and the two willows that her father had planted were now huge and drooping a deep shade across the driveway. It all looked so different and beautiful and for a moment hot moisture stung her eyes.

"It's so grown-up," she murmured.

"Things have a way of changing with time, Clementine."

Oh, yes, she understood that better than anyone, she thought wistfully.

After a moment, she said, "Well, guess we'd better go on up."

The drive up to the Jones house was less than a mile, but it seemed much farther. The road curved and climbed the whole distance and on either side of the rough track old twisted juniper stood like crippled warriors proudly hanging on to what little greenery they had left. The dirt was red and bare and some sort of sage was blooming pink and yellow. It was wild and beautiful scenery and Clementine wondered what it would be like to live here again, to see the fresh blue sky and breathe in the clean, crisp air of the high desert.

*Don't even think about it, Clementine. If you stayed your problems would eventually follow you. And then where would you be? Your staying might even put your old friends in danger.*

Shaking that grim notion away, she gripped the wheel and tried to focus on the huge potholes scattered here and there on the deteriorated road. Finally the pathway flattened out to a level spot some several feet below the house. Clementine parked her car to one side so that Quito would have ample room, then climbed out to the ground.

As she waited for him to join her, she stared up at the huge structure where she and her parents had once lived in.

By Houston standards, the place really wasn't anything to brag about. But in this area it was considered majestic, and had especially been admired eleven years ago when her father, Wilfred Jones, had it built.

The house was hacienda style with stuccoed walls in yellow-beige, a red tiled roof, and a long, ground level porch with arched supports running along the front. At the back of the structure an upstairs housed two more bedrooms to add to those on the ground floor. Off the second floor a large sundeck had been built of treated redwood. It was a spot where Clementine had often donned a bikini and lain in the warm sun.

Walking up behind her, Quito lifted his gaze toward the empty house. "Looks like you've been lucky. No vandalism. Which is surprising for as long as this place has been empty."

"Daddy still has the place equipped with an alarm system. I'm sure that's helped."

"Yeah, that and the fact that most young people are too lazy to walk all the way up here from the highway."

"Let's go take a look around," she said and without looking to see if he was following, she started up the twenty-five steps that would eventually take her to the front door.

As she climbed, memories assailed her. Some of them sweet and special, others painful. She tried not to think of any of those times now. It didn't do a person any good to keep going back to the past, she told herself. But for all these years her thoughts had lingered here with Quito.

Glancing over her shoulder, she noticed he was coming at a much slower pace and she suddenly remembered his injuries.

Skipping four steps down to him, she took hold of his arm. "Quito, I'm sorry. This is winding you. Maybe you shouldn't go the rest of the way."

He tossed her a dry look. "I'm all right. Hell, after this I should be able to run the 220."

She sighed. "I wasn't thinking about your injuries," she apologized again.

Shaking his head, he urged her on up the steps. "I'm not an invalid, Clementine. Maybe a little slow still, but it's going to take a damn sight more than a bastard with a nine millimeter to kill me."

Clementine didn't know what she would have done if she'd arrived in Aztec to find that Quito had been killed. Dear God, she couldn't begin to imagine the world without his powerful presence. Even eleven years ago, he'd been one of the driving forces that held this county together. She figured things were still that way. No doubt the people around here adored him and would have grieved at his passing. And she…well, she would have sunk into a black hole.

In spite of his determined words, she continued to hold on to his arm and they took each step slowly together until they reached the porch.

Sliding off her sunglasses, she dug into her shoulder bag until she felt the key ring. Once she'd unlocked the door and swung it open, she glanced around to see Quito standing just behind her. But his gaze wasn't on her. He was staring down at the valley spread below them.

"Will liked being up here on the mountain," Quito mused aloud. "How is your father now? And your mother?"

Tender emotion knotted her throat, forcing her to swallow before she could answer. "They're both doing fine. They live in Houston, not far from my place. Right now they've gone to spend the summer in Rome. Daddy didn't care a whit about going. But Mother loves it there and well, you know, Mother gets what Mother wants."

His lips twisted to a wry slant. "I never thought of your mother as demanding."

Clementine laughed softly. "You're being kind, Quito. We both know she's demanding and Daddy spoils her rotten. Just like he did—"

"You?"

Her blue gaze clashed with his dark brown eyes and she felt her stomach go weak as if she'd been punched by a fist.

Releasing a heavy breath, she murmured, "Yes, like me."

Before he could say more, she quickly turned and stepped inside. Dust and stale air assaulted her nose and she sneezed, then sneezed again.

As she punched off the alarm system, Quito said, "Bless you."

Glancing over her shoulder she saw that he'd followed her inside and the gentle expression on his face surprised her and warmed her spirits at the same time.

"Thank you, Quito," she said, then with a broad smile, she walked back to him and grabbed his hand.

"Come on," she said, tugging him along. "Let's go exploring."

The foyer was ridiculously large. Once they'd left it, they stepped into the great room. It was long and wide with huge pane windows that looked out over the valley floor. At night, they could see the lights of Bloomfield vying for a place among the stars shining across the desert.

It had once been a festive room where her mother

and father had held many parties and get-togethers. Now, except for the furniture covered in dust protectors, the place was ghostly quiet.

"I remember your mother had one of the most beautiful Christmas trees I'd ever seen standing over there in the corner. It reached the ceiling and she had gold ribbons tied on it and little toy soldiers hanging from the branches."

"Hmm. I remember, too. She gave you a tie with reindeer on it and a pair of green socks. I'm sure you thought she was crazy," Clementine said with a smile.

Actually he'd been honored that Delta Jones had even thought of putting him on her Christmas list. He was not from their lofty social circle and he was half Navajo and half Hispanic on top of that. Other than his adopted parents, he'd had no family of his own. No deep roots to explain his heritage. Sure, he'd been dating the Joneses' daughter, but they'd seemed to understand that he was just a pastime for Clementine and not a serious love affair. Her parents had never considered him a threat to sweep her away to his life and they'd been right. When Will had retired and packed up to move back to Houston, Clementine had been right beside her parents, not Quito.

"Your mother was always nice to me," he told her. "So was your father. I'm glad to hear they're doing well. Does your father still own Jones Oil and Gas?"

Clementine started toward a hallway that would

lead them toward a den, a study and several bedrooms. Quito followed a step behind her and as she
looked around at the dusty walls and windows, he
looked at her.

Except for her curves being a little rounder and
fuller, she still looked the same. She was a tall
woman with long shapely legs and arms. Her skin
was the sort that tanned deeply and her light hair was
a striking contrast against her face. As were her vivid
blue eyes. He'd always thought of them as two pools
of blue ocean. Calm and serene and beautiful at
times, stormy at others.

"Yes," she answered. "Oscar Ramirez keeps everything pulled together and running smoothly. You
might remember him. The corporate lawyer who used
to come up here in the summer to do a little fishing?"

"I remember."

"Well, anyway, Daddy has him, and he takes the
burden of the business off his shoulders."

Quito mentally cursed as he realized he'd been
thinking about the pleasures of her body rather than
the words coming out of her mouth.

"Uh—sorry, I didn't catch what you said," he allowed.

She glanced around at him and frowned. "Oh, I'll
bet you're getting tired. Let's go up to the sun deck
and rest a while before we start back," she suggested.
"Can you make the climb?"

Damn it, he'd always had the reputation of being as strong as a bull. It irked him to be less than a hundred percent in front of this woman. Still, her show of concern surprised him. It also made him feel special. A word he shouldn't link with Clementine. He wasn't special to her. He was simply an old lover.

The two of them climbed the stairs and entered the bedroom on the left. The bed and matching furniture were still in place and Clementine trailed a finger through the thick dust on the dresser top. "It would be nice to see everything clean again," she said wistfully. "Maybe I'll do that before I leave."

*Leave.* Of course she would be leaving in a short time, he thought. That shouldn't surprise him. It shouldn't make him feel like a dead, hollow log, either.

To the left of the bed, a wide, sliding glass door led onto the redwood sun deck. Quito unlatched the locks holding the glass in place, then slid it open.

A warm, fresh breeze met them as they stepped onto the wooden deck and Clementine lifted her face to the wind and shook back her hair.

"Leave the door open, Quito. Fresh air is what the whole house needs."

He left the door ajar as she requested and followed her to the middle of the large sundeck. On the north side of the house the lofty view looked down upon a large kidney-shaped swimming pool. On the opposite side, you could see all the way to the Navajo reservation. At the moment, the reds and greens and purples of the desert landscape shimmered in the morning sunshine.

Drawn by the view, Clementine walked over to the railing and was about to place her hands on the smooth wood when Quito called out.

"Don't touch that!"

Frozen by his command, she glanced over her shoulder at him. "Why?" she asked with a puzzled frown. "What's wrong?"

Quito walked over to her and nudged her back from the railing. "The weather could have loosened it. Let me check before you lean your weight on it."

He tested the sturdiness of the balustrade with a shake of his strong hand. To his satisfaction, it didn't budge.

"Looks okay," he told her. "Go ahead and lean all you want."

She moved up to the wooden rail and placed both hands around the smooth wood. For the umpteenth time since he'd ran into her, he noticed there was no wedding ring on her left hand. On her right hand there was a pear-shaped solitaire diamond the color of champagne and the size of too-many-karats-to-count.

On many women the ring would have looked gaudy, but on Clementine it looked perfect. She'd been born to be adorned and pampered and it showed in the proud carriage of her body.

He walked up beside her and leaned his hip against the deck railing. "So what have you been doing all these years, Clementine?"

She didn't answer immediately nor did she turn her head to the side to glance at him. Quito got the feeling she didn't want to share such personal information with him. And he was about to tell her that she didn't have to tell him anything when she spoke.

"I can tell you that I haven't been nearly as productive as you, Quito."

He frowned. "What does that mean?"

"You've made something of yourself." She turned slightly to look at him and he saw that her eyes were shadowed with secrets and grief. "You're a respected sheriff. You're doing exactly what you want to do."

"And you're not?" he asked gently.

She made a tiny sound in her throat that was something between a laugh and a moan. "Uh, I don't know that I've ever really done what I wanted to do."

"Clementine."

He said her name in a soft, scolding way and she looked at him with a pained smile. "Forget I said that, Quito. I guess you could say I've been busy. I worked for my father's company up until I was twenty-five, then I married a businessman from Houston. That lasted nearly five years. The past couple of years, I've been traveling abroad, donating my labor and money to needy children in war-torn countries."

To hear that she'd been married kicked him like a mule. But to know that she was now divorced sent a surge of wicked relief rushing through him. As for Clementine volunteering to the needy, he couldn't imagine it. Not that she wasn't generous. She was. He'd often heard her and her parents talk about giving to different charities. But to rough it in a third world country would take a mentally and physically tough person.

"You mean, you've been doing work like they do in the Peace Corps?" he asked incredulously.

One corner of her full lips curled upward. "Hard to believe, isn't it? Me washing clothes in a galvanized tub on a rub board and handing out food and medicine to people who rarely see a white woman."

Quito's eyes slipped up and down her tall figure. She was slender, but there was also a fit look about her that said she hadn't just been sitting on a couch eating chocolates. His eyes darted to her hands and this time he noticed her nails were cut short.

"Actually, it is. I can't see you living in some dirt hut in the jungle."

She laughed softly and he could see that surprising him had pleased her greatly. "I've been in jungles and deserts, mountains and cities, doing all sorts of work with my own two hands."

"Why? You could just donate money," he reasoned.

She shook her head and the sunlight rippled over her blond hair. "Not for me. Giving money isn't the same as giving of yourself. And anyway, after the divorce, I wanted to get away from Houston."

"A bad parting?" His eyes darted over her elusive expression.

Bad, Clementine thought with a strong urge to let out a mocking laugh. Her parting with Niles Westcott had been worse than bad, the divorce had been horrendous and now, well, she lived in fear every day of her life.

"Terrible. The only thing good about it was that there were no children to hurt."

He was quiet for a long time and then he asked, "Why no children? I thought you always said you wanted to have several children?"

Clementine could no longer look at him. The pain in her heart had to be showing in her eyes and she couldn't let him see. She couldn't let him guess what a mess she'd made of her life.

Looking down at the valley stretching before them, she sighed. "That's true. I did want children. But Niles turned out to be a far different man than I thought. I didn't want to have a child with him. He would have made a horrible father."

"Damn it all, Clementine. If that's the way you felt, then why did you marry the man?"

A tear slipped from her eye and she wiped it away as she turned her head to look at him. "Because I thought I was doing the right thing."

He shook his head and then he simply looked at her as though he couldn't decide whether he wanted to curse or cuddle her.

Finally he moved a step closer and Clementine's heart began to pound out of control.

"You thought you were doing the right thing when you walked away from me," he murmured.

With a muffled cry, she suddenly stepped forward and buried her face in the middle of his chest.

"Forgive me, Quito. Please forgive me."

## Chapter Three

His fingers pushed into her silky hair and he stroked the back of her head soothingly.

"Clementine, whatever you're thinking, I don't hate you. I've never hated you." He bent his head and pressed his cheek against the top of her head. "You were very young then. And there's no need to rehash the past now. Just because we were once lovers doesn't mean we can't be friends now. Hmm?"

Clementine wanted to slip her arms around him and hold him for long, long moments. She wanted to breathe in that remembered scent of his skin and hair, feel the strength of his arms curling around her.

But she couldn't invite or provoke any sort of affection from this man. She loved him too much to make his life miserable a second time.

After a minute or so, his forefinger came under her chin and he tilted her face up to his. Clementine blinked the moisture from her eyes and struggled to smile at him.

"Of course we can be friends, Quito. I'd like that very much."

"Good. I'd like it, too."

Her eyes slid to his mouth and her stomach began to flutter as though the wings of thousands of birds were taking flight inside of her.

"Uh, maybe we'd better go down now," she told him. "I'm sure you're getting tired."

Their eyes met and she licked her lips. Quito cleared his throat and stepped back.

"Yeah. It's time I got back to town. Or my deputies will be sending out a search party."

The two of them stepped back into the bedroom and Quito latched the sliding door behind him. After they'd gone downstairs and were about to leave the foyer, Quito asked, "What are you going to do with the place? Sell it?"

Clementine finished cuing in the alarm system, then opened the door.

"I'm not sure. I came up here with intentions of putting it on the market. But now that I see it, I don't know, it still seems like home. Doesn't that sound silly? It's been eleven years since I stepped foot on the place, yet in many ways it seems like only yesterday."

Quito couldn't admit to her that it felt the same way to him. Each time he looked at Clementine, it felt as if nothing had changed. No years had passed. He felt like he still had the right to pull her into his arms and kiss her as many times as he wanted. But he had to remember that everything had changed.

"Well, you did live here for three years," he reasoned.

"Yes, but compared to eleven that's not very many," she replied.

The two of them left the porch and walked down the long wide steps that would take them off the cliff side and onto the flat, parking area.

Quito made the trip going down much more easily and when they reached the vehicles she was relieved to see that his breathing seemed normal.

"It's obvious you're not staying here," Quito said as they walked to her car first. "Did you find a place in town?"

She nodded. "The Apache Junction Hotel. But who knows, I might clean up part of this place and stay for a few days." She glanced wistfully around her. "It would be nice to vacation in the cooler, dryer air for a while. When I left Houston, the city was under a hurricane watch." And not just from the weather, either, she thought, grimly.

She'd heard from the little birds she kept on lookout that Niles had been hunting everywhere for her. Thankfully he hadn't learned that she'd gone to Afghanistan and her time there had been relatively peaceful. She only wished she could have a few days here in San Juan county before he caught on to her trail.

"There's nothing stopping you from staying is there?" he asked.

She swallowed hard as he reached down and opened the car door for her. "No. Not really," she lied. "I do have another trip planned soon to South America, some of the mountain villages there. This time I'm hoping to get a driver and a truck full of food and medicine through the bandits that control the areas. We tried once before and they stopped us with machine guns and forced us to hand the goods over to them."

"Hell fire, Clementine, you could be killed going off on such ventures," he cursed.

She slid behind the steering wheel, then lifted a steady gaze to his.

"I could get killed in Houston, too."

He frowned and sensing he was going to start asking her questions that she didn't want to answer, she started the engine.

Quito shut the door to the sleek black, sports car and stepped back. "Will I see you again before you leave?"

It wouldn't be wise. She would eventually pay for these few minutes she'd spent with him this morning. The short time was already burned into her memory and once she returned to Houston, she would relive them over and over like a spinster reliving her first and only kiss.

"I don't know," she said thoughtfully. "Do you want to?"

A devilish smile suddenly crooked his mouth and he bent his head through the open window and kissed her.

The intimate contact had been the last thing she expected. And for a moment she was stunned motionless as his lips made a gentle foray over hers and then slowly, her mouth opened and her hand came up to cup the side of his face.

How could it be that the taste of him, the feel of his lips were so sweetly the same? she wondered. And how could it be that she still wanted him so badly?

By the time he pulled his head back slightly from hers, she could feel her pulse beating wildly in her temples, like a drum warning her to stop, stop, stop.

"What do you think?" he asked.

She thought he was moving way too fast. She even thought he might be trying to make of fool of her, to hurt her for walking away all those years ago. But Quito had never been a spiteful person and there didn't seem to be any hidden motives in his eyes, only a bit of lust.

"All right," she said with a sheepish smile. "I'll take you out for dinner tomorrow night. Can you make it?"

Smiling, he stepped back from the car. "You can call me at the office," he told her. "I'm usually there until six."

She nodded then waved goodbye and raised the window. Thankfully the glass was tinted darkly and hid the worried expression on her face as she drove away.

The next morning Quito was sitting at his desk signing off on a request for two arrest warrants when his secretary, Juliet, buzzed the intercom. "Sir, Dr. Hastings is on line two. Can you speak with her?"

Quito frowned. The under sheriff's wife was a medical doctor and had a thriving practice in a small clinic just a few blocks away from the department. Although she'd been a longtime friend, he couldn't imagine why she would want to speak to him this morning. Unless she wanted to talk to him about Jess.

"Yes, I'll get it, Juliet." He reached for the phone. "Good morning, Victoria. What gives me the pleasure of hearing your voice this morning?"

"Hi, Quito. I know you're busy, but I'm keeping a promise. Your doctor in Farmington called and asked if I would give you a checkup. He's leaving town and won't be back for a couple of weeks. Apparently your checkup was due today, is that right?"

"Hell, I don't know. Just a minute." He flipped

open an appointment book. "Yeah. Here it is. It's this afternoon. Juliet would have probably reminded me, but I'd forgotten."

Victoria chuckled. "That's what we have secretaries for, Quito." She paused, then said, "Let's see, it looks like this morning I've got a space between patients. Can you be over here in fifteen minutes?"

Quito straightened up in his chair. "You really weren't kidding?"

"Of course I wasn't kidding. Did you think this was just a ploy to get you over here so I could see your chest?" she teased.

"That's just it. Jess might not like you looking at me in such a—personal way."

Victoria laughed again. "I've got a news flash for you, Quito. Jess knows that I look at men's bodies every day. He's used to it. Now quit making excuses and get over here."

"Okay. Okay. I'll be there. But I don't like it."

"You don't have to like it," she cheerily replied, then promised, "I'll try to end your suffering as quickly as I can."

Quito assured her that she'd see him in a few minutes, then hung up the phone.

By car, the doctor's office was less than two minutes away. When he entered the clinic there were several patients seated in the outer waiting room. He walked over to the receptionist, expecting her to tell him to have a seat and wait like the rest, but instead she jerked her thumb toward the back where the examination rooms were located.

"Go on back to Room 2, Sheriff. She's waiting on you."

He found Victoria in the square, sterile looking room. The tall brunette was dressed in a white lab coat and standing at a small counter scribbling something on a chart. When she looked up, she smiled at him.

"I wish all my patients were this prompt," she said and gestured toward the examining table. "Have a seat, Quito, get comfortable and remove your shirt. This isn't going to hurt."

He unbuttoned his shirt and slipped it off his shoulders as she adjusted the earpieces of her stethoscope.

"Maybe not," he said. "But it's silly. Dr. Holloway knows I'm on the mend. What is there to look at anyway?"

"Be quiet and let me listen," she ordered as she wrapped a blood pressure cuff around his arm.

Victoria Hastings was a young, beautiful woman and as she thumped and probed and ordered him to breathe deeply, he could only wonder why it was that she, nor any other woman, ever affected him the way Clementine did. Why did he only feel that pull of attraction when he thought about or looked upon the blond Texas beauty?

Eventually Victoria put away her stethoscope and

handed him his shirt. "Okay, Sheriff Perez, you're finished. I pronounce you fit."

He looked at her with surprise. "You mean, I can go off light duty now? I can do anything I want?"

Her smile turned wry. "Within reason," she said. "Just don't try to tear out any old fence posts. Or ride a bucking bronc. On the other hand, you should be walking as much as you can to help your lungs get back to full strength."

"I'll try," he told her as he buttoned his shirt.

"You're a lucky man, Quito. A lesser man would have died from the wounds you suffered."

He shook his head. "I'm not any tougher than the next guy, Victoria. It was all those candles that were lit for me. All the prayers said."

Smiling, she patted him on the shoulder. "I think you're probably right, Quito." She looked at him with thoughtful concern. "How have you been doing otherwise? Nightmares? Trouble sleeping?"

"It's getting better," he said. Although, he didn't admit to lying awake most of the night last night. That problem had occurred because his mind had been consumed with Clementine, not the thug who'd shot him full of holes.

"I can prescribe something for you if you need it. Just let me know," she offered. "Or if you need to talk to someone other than a man wearing a badge, just pick up the phone and call me."

He nodded. "Thanks, Victoria. I'll remember that."

She folded her arms across her chest and looked at him with renewed interest. "Uh, now that we've got the medical stuff out of the way, I heard through the grapevine that Clementine Jones is back in town. Is that right?"

His gaze slipped to the toes of his black cowboy boots. "Yeah. That's right."

"Have you seen her yet?"

He nodded. "We spent a little time together yesterday," he admitted. He lifted his gaze back to Victoria. "Have you seen her?"

Victoria shook her head. "No. Where is she staying? Out at the Jones house?"

"No. She's at the Apache Junction."

Frowning, Victoria said, "That's not necessary. I'll see if she wants to come out to the ranch and stay with us while she's here. Uh, how long does she plan to stay?"

The question caused him to stiffen inside, but he tried to sound as casual as he could as he answered, "I don't know. Probably not long."

Victoria's brows lifted ever so slightly and Quito wanted to curse. The woman was just too sharp. No doubt she'd picked up on the tinge of bitterness in his voice.

Her expression suddenly grew empathetic. "I'm sure seeing her again was tough on you."

Quito did his best to appear cool. That's the way a lawman had to be when he was under fire.

He released a long, weary breath. "A little. But it was good to see her, too. I'm glad she's come back. I think it was about time."

Victoria studied him thoughtfully. "So you've always expected her to return someday?"

Had he? In the deepest part of him, he knew he would see her again one day. He'd just not known how long it would be before she came back to this corner of New Mexico, back to the call of his heart.

"I did. Don't ask me why. But I did."

"Well, I won't ask you what this means to you. You probably don't even know yourself."

"Thanks, Victoria."

He was sliding off the examining table when nurse Nevada Ortiz knocked on the door and poked her head inside the room.

"Victoria, Mrs. Grayson is getting so irate about waiting on you that she's threatening to get dressed and go home."

The doctor tossed Quito an amused look. "Excuse me, Sheriff, I believe you know how it is to deal with irate citizens."

The two women quickly disappeared and Quito left the building feeling happy about his medical report, but troubled about his thoughts of Clementine. It didn't matter that he was still in love with the woman and had been for the past thirteen years. That was an affliction he would never get over. It was something he had to live with no matter if she was miles and miles away from him or just across the room.

He couldn't allow himself to start thinking, hoping that she would somehow change her mind and decide she wanted to live here with him. She'd been born into wealth. She didn't know any other lifestyle. If she tried to live here permanently, she'd be a fish out of water. And he'd be a sucker fish to think she could change.

When Quito returned to the building that housed his staff of lawmen and the jail, he stuck his head into Juliet's cubbyhole to collect any messages she might have taken for him, then quickly walked down the hallway to his office. The door was ajar and he was a little more than surprised to hear voices from inside.

Without bothering to knock, he entered the room and was taken aback to see Clementine sitting in the chair in front of his desk. And in his own chair Jess was leaning back with his boots crossed and a cup of coffee in his hand.

"Well, it's good to see you've been taking care of my office while I was away," he said to Jess.

Laughing, the under sheriff rose to his feet. "Sorry, Quito. Clementine wanted to see you so I brought her back here. I knew you wouldn't be long. My wife doesn't have time to dally around with her patients. Especially the male ones."

Rolling his eyes at Jess, he said, "You don't deserve that woman."

Jess chuckled. "I know it." As he started out of the room, he glanced at Clementine. "See if you can get him in a better mood, will you?"

She nodded in a conspiring way. "I'll do my best."

The under sheriff disappeared out the door and Quito walked over to where Clementine sat with her long bare legs crossed and an impish smile on her berry-colored lips.

"Jess has been catching me up on all the news around here."

"I'm sure. That was easier than handing you a copy of the *Aztec Gazette*."

His dry comment pulled a soft laugh from her, which only made Quito frown more.

"I'm not talking about that sort of news," she said. "I mean personal stuff. He told me that he and Victoria has been married for nearly two years now and that they have two children. A girl, Katrina, and a baby boy, Sam. He also told me that Ross got married, too. I always remembered him as the wild one of the Ketchum boys. I guess the years have settled him down."

"He has a beautiful Apache wife. I think she's settled him down more than the years," he said, then looked at her pointedly. "Are you here to chat about the social goings on of Aztec or was there some other reason?"

The smile fell from her face. "Boy, did they give you a shot over at the doctor's office? You're behaving like you've been jabbed with something."

Realizing he was sounding out of sorts, he let out a deep breath and lifted the gray Stetson from his head. Running a hand over his crow-black hair, he said, "Sorry. I've had a lot of distractions this morning."

Her blue eyes were full of concern as they flicked over him. "What did the doctor say? Are you healing?"

At least that was something he could be happy about, Quito thought. "She says I'm well enough to do pretty much anything I want."

A bright smile replaced the serious expression on Clementine's face. "That's wonderful news. So that means you're well enough to have a picnic."

Quito stared at her. "A picnic! Hell, Clem, I'm too old for that sort of thing."

She rose to her feet and Quito's breath lodged somewhere in the middle of his throat as her face came dangerously near to his.

"Old?" she murmured. "Quito, there's nothing about you that's old."

His nostrils flared as he drank in the flowery spices that scented her skin. "Uh, I thought you were going to take me out to dinner."

"I was. But I decided it would be nicer not to go to some busy restaurant where people would be staring. Even though it's been eleven years, I doubt that people have forgotten that we were an item. There'll be gossip everywhere that the old flames between us have burst to life again. That might hurt you politically and I wouldn't want that to happen."

Quito cursed. "What goes on between you and me is nobody's business but ours."

. She shrugged. "All right, if that's the way you feel. But I still want to have the picnic," she said cheerfully. "I thought we might drive up to the mountains and walk to the meadow. You remember the one with the willow trees, where we caught the trout?"

Remember? How could he forget? It was the spot where they'd made love for the very first time. Was she trying to kill him with memories or was she simply wanting to relive the past?

Either way, he should give her a flat-out no. He didn't want those old flames between them fanned for any reason. She'd already burned him badly. Much more from her and he'd be nothing more than a useless pile of ashes.

"I remember." Her blue eyes caught his and he felt his heart jump into a dangerous rhythm. "What time do you want for me to meet you?"

Smiling with pleasure, she grabbed both his hands and squeezed. "Don't worry about that. I'll pick you up here. What time?"

He felt wicked and indecent and stupid. But for the first time in years, he felt alive.

"Six."

She leaned forward and pressed a soft kiss upon his cheek. "I'll be here."

## Chapter Four

Later that evening, Quito was signing a request for additional funding for equipment when a soft knock sounded on his door.

Knowing it was Clementine, he picked up the document and switched off the light on his desk. Then reaching for his Stetson, he slapped it on and went to open the door.

She was standing on the other side, a soft smile on her face and a light in her blue eyes that stirred his imagination.

"Ready?" she asked.

He nodded. "Just let me drop this by Julie's office and then we'll be on our way."

She walked along beside him as they made their way down the wide corridor and the perfume she'd been wearing earlier drifted once again to his nostrils. She smelled sweet and lusty at the same time and he was amazed at the sexual urges suddenly stirring his body.

Three weeks ago, he'd been almost dead. On top of that, he had not seen this woman in eleven years. How could his body suddenly turn into a wild buck deer?

Outside on the sidewalk, she pointed to where her car was parked several spaces on down the street from the building. "I have everything loaded into the trunk," she told him. "Do you think we still have enough daylight to make it to the meadow?"

Rather than glance at his watch, Quito turned a narrowed eye on the ball of hot sun. "It will be nearly nine before darkness falls. We'll have time. But I don't think we should drive your car. Let's take my SUV," he suggested. "That way if we have to go over some rough spots, we'll have four-wheel drive."

She shrugged. "Sounds fine to me. But isn't that a department vehicle?"

He cast her a grin. "We're going up there on department business. I got a tip that someone left some robbery evidence up there. We might accidentally stumble over it."

Catching on to his real meaning, she smiled and looped her arm through his. "Then we'll be entirely legal. And no one can roast you over a fire."

Quito wasn't so sure he wasn't roasting right this minute. But he kept the thought to himself. It wouldn't do for Clementine to get the idea that she still had that much effect on him. No, he needed to play it cool. But how was he going to do that when every part of him was on a slow burn?

After loading the picnic things into Quito's SUV, they climbed in and he headed the vehicle north. For a little more than thirty minutes he drove the highway to Durango until they reached the foothills announcing bigger mountains to come.

Once Quito turned off the asphalt, the dim dirt road grew treacherous and Clementine held on to the armrests as the vehicle jostled from side to side.

"The place has certainly changed," Clementine commented as Quito wrestled with the steering wheel. "The road wasn't nearly this rough when we used to come up here."

"*Everything* changes, Clementine."

Darting a glance at him, she could only think how true his words were. These past years away from him had changed her in so many ways. She wanted to think she'd learned lessons and moved forward in her life in a positive manner, but sitting here with Quito made her wonder if she were stepping backward into a place where it would be impossible for her to exist.

Quito looked across to the woman buckled into the bucket seat. There was a tiny frown marring her forehead, a distant stare to her eyes. He didn't try to guess what she was thinking. Probably that she should have never suggested this little picnic trip, he thought. On the other hand, she might have Houston on her mind. No doubt she had a man there. He couldn't imagine a woman like her not being attached to some good-looking guy with a fat bank account. But he didn't want to think about that now. He'd never wanted to think about it.

"There's a spot not too far from here where the road widens. I think we'd better park and walk from there. Did you wear something reasonable on your feet?"

He glanced down to see if she was still wearing the stiletto heels, and Clementine lifted her foot to show him a plain brown cowboy boot.

She smiled coyly at him. "See. I've grown up and gotten a little common sense."

He grunted with amusement. "Only a little?" he asked.

A soft laugh slipped past her lips. "I have the wrong hair color to absorb a head full of common sense."

Maybe the rich girl from Houston hadn't changed all that much, Quito thought. At least she was still able to make fun of herself and she still liked to picnic. But there was something about her eyes, he thought. Something dark and desolate that made him want to take her into his arms, stroke her face and kiss her lips until her blue eyes were sparkling with life and passion as they used to.

For the next five minutes Quito wrestled the SUV over rough, steep terrain until the vehicle reached a flat slab of rock that crested over the bottom shelf of the mountain. Here the track they'd been following petered out and he parked the SUV safely to one side beneath a scraggly piñon pine.

Clementine had packed a large picnic hamper and filled an insulated carrier with ice, soda and water. Once Quito lifted the two items from the back seat, she reached to take the smaller one.

"Let me carry the sodas," she said. "You shouldn't be straining yourself."

He shot her an offended glance. "I'm not straining anything. You just walk along beside me and watch your step," he ordered. "You're not walking in a mall in Houston now."

Instead of raising her temper, his little jab only made her chuckle. "Oh, Quito, I'm walking on easy ground compared to some of the places I've been in the past two years."

He glanced at her again, only this time his dark brows were pulled together in a frown. "Sorry. I forgot about your volunteer work. I suppose you haven't exactly been walking on easy street."

*Nothing has been easy about my life since I left you.*

Clementine contained that revealing thought in the hollow part of her heart and instead said, "Not easy. But I've learned a lot about the world. And about myself."

"Like what?"

"Hmm. Well, that I can get along without luxuries and comforts if I have to. And that there's much more important things in life than having a career that makes you lots of money or having a social position in the community."

She sounded so sincere, Quito thought. And maybe she did really mean what she was saying. But it was easy for a person, who had money to burn, to talk as though they could easily do without it. "Uh, where do you live now?" he asked. "When you're not traveling. With your parents?"

Shaking her head, she said, "I haven't lived with my parents since—college. I have a house in the same neighborhood as my parents. But I rarely stay there. I don't like the city too much anymore, I feel stifled there."

God forgive me, she thought, as Quito silently walked along beside her. She was trying to be as honest as she could be and everything she'd told him was the truth. Except the part about the city making her feel stifled. When it wasn't really the city at all. It was Niles and his constant attempts to have all sorts of connections with her. Attempts that frankly had become downright frightening. But she didn't want Quito to know that. She didn't want him to know what an utter mess she'd made of her life. And how poor her judgment in men had been.

She could feel him glance at her and she gave him a faint smile. "What's wrong?" she asked as she spotted the dour look on his face.

"Nothing. I was just thinking, wondering why you suddenly decided to come back to San Juan County."

"Why?" she asked with a faint grin. "Does it upset you to be having a picnic with a divorced woman?"

"I'd be more upset if you were married," he said simply.

"If I were a married woman I wouldn't be here with you. I think you know I'm not that sort."

He nodded. "Yes. I know it," he said, then gestured ahead of them. "Now, look out there."

Peeping around a pine bough for a better look, Clementine gasped. "Oh, Quito, it's beautiful!"

She rushed forward a few steps, then stopped to take it all in. The meadow, their meadow, as she'd always thought of it, was in full bloom. Yellow and pink buttercups and wild red clover created a vibrant blanket across the small, grassy area.

Quito came to stand next to her. "The snowfall was heavy this past winter. It's made the flowers beautiful this spring."

Clementine didn't want to think about the nitrogen in the snow or any other scientific reason for the beauty before her. She'd rather think Mother Nature made it this special just for her and Quito.

Sighing with pleasure, she drank in the azure-blue sky and the gorgeous carpet of blossoms. If only her days could stay this beautiful and peaceful, she thought longingly.

"Come on," Quito urged. "Let's go down by the stream to eat."

The two of them walked across the edge of the meadow and climbed over several boulders that lined the trickling stream making its way down the mountain. Here, along the water's edge, globe willows and small cottonwoods grew. Their shade cooled the quiet spot and Clementine smiled with delight as she sat down cross-legged on the ground.

"Sorry. I didn't bring a blanket. Only a small tablecloth," she told Quito. "We can put our supper out on it, but we'll have to sit on the ground and dirty our jeans."

He placed the basket and the container of drinks on the square of fabric, then eased himself down a small space away from her.

"A little dirt never hurt me," he said. "Besides, I'm

starving. I'd almost be willing to sit in a prickly pear patch to get something in my stomach."

She glanced at him as she reached to open the picnic hamper. "Still a man with a big appetite, I see," she said with a faint smile. "I hope you're not disappointed with fried chicken. I wanted a traditional picnic with chicken and potato salad and baked beans."

His brows lifted in question. "I hope you got the food from the Wagon Wheel."

Smiling happily, she said, "It is. That waitress friend of yours, Betty, put it all together for me. She said she hoped you enjoy it"

Quito groaned. "You told Betty about this?"

Clementine looked at him, her heart pounding with unexplained dread. "I didn't know it should be a secret. Uh, is there a woman that you don't want knowing about our picnic?"

Quito rolled his eyes. "Not hardly. There hasn't been—" He stopped abruptly as he realized he wasn't ready to admit to Clementine that, since her, he'd not had any deep relationship with a woman. She didn't need to know what a hold she'd had on him back then. Or what a hold she still had on his heart.

"No. There's no woman. I wouldn't be here with you if there was," he said, using the very words she'd used on him earlier.

"Good. Now that we've got that out of the way," she said, "let's eat. I'm starving, too."

He helped her smooth out the tablecloth and place all the small plastic containers of food onto the makeshift table. At the bottom of the basket, along with paper plates and plastic utensils, he found a bottle of wine and two plastic goblets. The discovery had him looking up at her in surprise.

"What's this for?" he asked.

Her cheeks flushed a pretty pink as she shrugged and smiled. "I thought it would be nice to have a little toast."

"To what?" he asked guardedly.

She glanced over at the sparkling clear water racing over small boulders and pooling in a wide, dished-out basin not far from where the two of them were sitting. "To having dinner together again. To being here again in our meadow."

Quito didn't miss the word *our* but he tried his best not to make too much of it. Clementine was only here for a few days. She belonged in Houston or some place where there were bright lights, excitement, art, cultural entertainment, and lots of money. Not in a little desert town like Aztec.

"I haven't been up here in a long time," he admitted while looking around him. A couple of magpies were fluttering among the tree limbs shading a portion of the stream, their musical chatter was the only sound around, except for the loud heartbeat in his ears and it seemed to be getting faster by the minute.

Damn it, he didn't know what was wrong with him. He was too old for this sort of thing. Picnicking in the mountains, sitting on the ground and gazing at a beautiful woman who'd once torn his heart into pieces. There were plenty of reasons he shouldn't be here. But he'd never had common sense where Clementine was concerned and apparently the past eleven years hadn't changed that part of him.

Sighing, Clementine lifted her gaze to the late evening sky. "It's so beautiful here. So peaceful. I've thought about this place often." She leveled her gaze back on his dark face. "And you," she added softly.

Something tightened the muscles in his throat, forcing him to look away from her and swallow hard. "And what were you thinking?" he asked a bit dryly. "Wonder what ol' hayseed Quito is doing back in Aztec?"

A frown wrinkled her otherwise smooth features and as Quito turned his gaze back on her he felt time peeling away and once again he was that young, new sheriff and Clementine was a beautiful innocent with eyes full of promise that beckoned more than the curl of a finger ever could. She'd been a virgin when the two of them had made love here in the meadow and though he'd felt badly afterward about taking her innocence, she'd sworn how glad she was that it had been him to initiate her into womanhood.

Quito had been in love with her even before that first encounter. But their union here in the meadow had sealed his fate as far as matters of the heart were concerned. He'd never wanted anyone as much as he'd wanted Clementine. And the years hadn't changed that for him. Looking back on it now, he marveled that she hadn't gotten pregnant with his child. The two of them had made love every time they'd had the chance to be together and neither of them had bothered to worry about birth control. Quito could only wonder how things might have gone if she had gotten pregnant. Maybe she would have stayed and married him. Or maybe she would have walked away with his baby and allowed some other, wealthy man to raise it.

"Quito! That's an awful thing to say. Never in my life have I thought of you as hayseed." She scowled at him. "And why are you frowning? What are you thinking?"

He shook his head and reached for a can of soda. Popping the lid, he said a bit sharply. "Nothing. I'm just hungry. Let's eat."

She watched him take a long swallow and once he lowered it, she reached across the small space between them and wrapped her fingers around his bare forearm. His skin was warm and the muscle and bone beneath her touch was hard. She felt herself melting, longing to push her hand upward onto his shoulder, to circle his neck with her arms and crush her breasts against his broad chest.

The wanting was an ache inside her, an ache that had lasted throughout the years they'd been apart.

"Quito, I'm sorry if coming here has made you unhappy," she said softly. "I thought it would be nice for both of us."

His nostrils flared as his dark eyes slipped slowly, questioningly over her face. "Don't you understand, Clem, what it's doing to me to be here with you like this? All I can think of is how much I wanted you."

Her heart tripped wildly as she inched her hand slowly up his arm. "That's all I can think about, too."

His gaze slipped pointedly to her hand then back to her face and he looked at her with a bit of longing, anger and confusion all rolled up together.

Clementine purposely pushed the containers of food from the space between them, then scooted closer so that her thigh was touching his and her hands could rest upon his chest.

"I didn't plan this picnic to seduce you, Quito. But right now it seems like a very good idea."

She leaned toward him, her lips parted, her eyes begging. Quito couldn't have resisted her even if he'd been drawing in his last breath of life.

With a muffled oath of self-disgust, he wrapped his arms around her shoulders and pulled her to him. "Damn it, Clementine, what do you think I am, an idiot?"

One hand came up to touch his cheek and she watched his eyelids lower just a fraction as the pads of her fingers traced the length of his jaw. "I don't get the urge to kiss idiots," she whispered.

Roughly his fingers pushed into her hair until they were cradling the back of her head and tilting the curves of her mouth up to his.

"Come here. Come here, my darling Clementine."

The sweet words were spoken against her lips and by the time her name whispered away on the breeze he was kissing her the way he used to kiss her—hot and all consuming.

Groaning deep in her throat, Clementine shifted her hips onto his lap and circled his neck with her arms. The position brought them even closer together and before either realized what was happening, Quito was easing her down to the ground.

She felt the cool bed of river pebbles beneath her back, but only in an absent way. Her senses, her thoughts were completely focused on the only man she'd ever loved.

As his lips finally left hers to nuzzle a trail along the side of her neck, she murmured, "Quito. Quito. I didn't know this was going to happen. But I wanted it to. Don't hate me for that."

Easing his head back, he looked at her with an expression of wry surrender. "Does it feel like I hate you?"

A helpless moan sounded deep in her throat. "It feels like we've never been apart."

Quito's hand pushed at the silken blond hair that had dipped across her cheek. The skin of his fingers was tough and rasped ever so slightly against her skin as he drew his hand across her forehead.

"I know."

It was all he could say. His throat was too thick as powerful emotions suddenly took away his ability to speak, to think, to do anything but lean his head downward and drink from the lips he'd constantly dreamed about.

On and on, he kissed her as they both grew oblivious to the falling sun and the lengthening shadows. The more their mouths refused to part, the more Clementine began to burn with a desperate desire—a fact which shocked her completely. For a long time now, her body had refused to react to any man with any sort of pleasure or interest. It was incredible how instantly Quito had cured her of that problem.

"Clem, we…uh…I think we'd better stop this," he finally said in a ragged voice.

"No! Quito, I—" She tightened her arms around him, desperate to keep him by her side.

Closing his eyes, he leaned his forehead against hers. "We can't do this here, Clem."

"Why? I can't think of any other place I'd rather do it," she told him.

His dark eyes opened and he studied her face for only moments before he pushed himself to his feet, then reached down for her hand.

Wordlessly she placed her hand in his and after he'd pulled her to a standing position they left the side of the stream and walked to a spot in the meadow where they were knee deep in flowers.

With the scent of wild blossoms drifting all around them, Quito lay her down in the grass and flowers and began to unbutton the white cotton blouse she was wearing.

"I don't care why you're doing this," Quito muttered more to himself than to her. "And I'm not going to ask."

"I hope you're doing this because you want me," she replied as she watched his big fingers fumble with the buttons.

Want her? Quito had wanted her for so many years now that he wouldn't know what it was like *not* to want her.

"I'm better at showing than telling," he said thickly.

After that, Clementine helped him ease apart the last of the buttons, then lifted her shoulders from the ground so that he could pull the blouse away from her. When his hands immediately went to her breasts, she arched against him like a cat just begging for the stroke of his hand.

He gave her that and so much more as he did away with her lacy bra, then brought his lips down over one hardened nipple.

The fact that they were making love in the light of day and in a secluded meadow was enough to push Clementine's senses to a high point. But being back in Quito's arms after years of emotional drought was making her whole body explode with remembered pleasure.

Quito's need must have been as deep and urgent as hers, because he shimmied her blue jeans down her long legs and followed them with her lacy panties.

When the heel of his hand finally pushed against the wet ache between her thighs, she was desperate for him to enter her.

Writhing from one side to the other, she begged, "Hurry, Quito. Don't make me wait. Please!"

Poised over her, he paused long enough to ask, "Are you protected, Clementine? Because I'm sure as hell not carrying a condom."

His roughly asked question didn't deter her. Rather, she brought her hands against his back to urge him down over her. "It's okay. I take the pill. There won't be a problem."

Maybe not where pregnancy was concerned, Quito thought. But what about his mental state? What about the ache in his body that would go on and on, even long after she was gone?

It didn't matter how his mind answered the questions, he decided. He was already in such a grip of desire, he couldn't turn away from her. Flames were eating at his loins and pushing heated blood to every part of his body. Good or bad, having her was the only way to end his misery.

He positioned himself over her and as he fumbled with the zipper on his jeans, she wrapped her long legs around his with urgent anticipation.

"Damn it, Clem, this is crazy! But I want you. Want—you!"

The last of his words were muffled by a guttural groan as he pushed his heated shaft into the moist folds of her body.

"Oh, Quito, I want you, too. I've missed you so much. So much," she whispered frantically as her hips lifted to meet his urgent thrust.

He wouldn't allow himself to think about what she was saying. He didn't want his heart to experience the same joy his body was feeling, but with Clementine it was difficult to keep the two of them separate and before long he'd lost himself to her completely as his body rocked with hers.

Clementine was certain the two of them had jetted backward in time. Nothing had changed. Their bodies fit together as if they were born for each other.

And instead of feeling awkward about their unexpected reunion, she felt the wild, sweet pleasure of coming home.

His lips and hands were touching her in spots that had lain dead and neglected for far too long. She shivered with longing, even as her flesh heated and sweat began to glisten her skin.

Before long she could feel his strokes deepen and quicken and her own body tightened in anticipation. His teeth sank into the side of her neck and she cried out with reckless pleasure.

"Love me, Quito. Love me!"

Her voice was coming from a far distance as Quito grasped her buttocks and groaned mindlessly as he spilled himself inside her. And almost instantly he could feel her tightening around him as her hips ground against his.

For long moments their bodies continued to rock and sway with the give and take of their hungry needs. Then Quito finally collapsed on top of her, his face buried between her breasts, his hands still clutching her hips.

Long moments passed before Quito could roll away from her. Clementine shifted onto her side and propped her head upon her hand as she gazed across the few inches separating their faces. A tight grimace was gripping his features and she immediately reached out to him in concern.

"Dear God, Quito, are you all right? Did I hurt you?"

"I thought it was the man that was supposed to ask that question," he mumbled crossly. "And I'm not an invalid."

Leaning her upper body over him, she gently wiped the sweat from his brow. "I didn't accuse you of being an invalid. And quit all your worrying about being macho in front of me. You've been seriously injured and I forgot in the heat of the moment. Did I hurt your ribs?"

She rubbed her fingers lightly up and down the left side of his rib cage. The bullets he'd taken had left blue jagged scars upon his dark skin. She gently stroked the welts of healing flesh while thanking God the damage hadn't taken his life.

"Only a little," he answered.

"I'm so sorry," she whispered, then bending her head, she kissed him softly on the mouth. "I only want to give you pleasure, Quito."

Her long hair slipped forward to create a blond curtain around her face. Reaching up, he pinned the silky strands back to her shoulders so that he could see her eyes.

"You did. And I thank you."

The corners of her lips tilted to a sexy grin. "My pleasure, Sheriff."

She was treating this whole thing as though it was the most natural thing in the world for the two of them to be making love. And he figured it would be best if he could treat it the same way. After all, it wasn't to be taken seriously. Clementine had simply gotten the urge to have sex and he'd been too weak to resist her.

"Uh, I think we'd better get up. The sun is almost down and we haven't eaten yet."

Sitting up, Clementine looked toward the west where low mountains hid the last bit of an orange sun. "You're right. But—" Twisting around, she ran her hand across his hard stomach. "I could forget about eating, if you could."

Grimacing, he zipped his jeans and pushed himself to a sitting position. "I happen to be starving. And I think we need to let our heads cool. And clear."

A pained expression filled her eyes as she placed her hands on his shoulders to halt his movements. "Quito," she said with soft disappointment, "please don't regret what just happened. I think it was wonderful. And I think—" She reached up and stroked a forefinger against his cheek. "That it was wonderful for you, too."

Closing his eyes, he turned his face to one side. The breath he heaved from his lungs told her he was upset even before he spoke a word. "I'm not dead yet, Clementine. I can enjoy sex with a woman."

Hurt by his cynical tone, especially after what they'd just shared, she dropped her hand and eased back from him. Of course it had been sex between them. She couldn't call it love. They'd been apart too long. And to think that Quito could ever love her again, would be darn foolish on her part. She'd smashed any hope of being loved by him when she'd hightailed it back to Houston.

"Well, thank God for that," she said, determined not to make it an issue. "If that bullet had been a bit lower you might have wound up impotent. And no doubt that would have left a lot of women around here very unhappy."

He looked at her, rolled his eyes, then grunted a laugh. "A lot of women? Just a handful is more like it."

And Clementine already hated them all. She couldn't bear to think that any woman, other than her, had spent time in Quito's arms. But she had to stop and remind herself that she'd left him a free man. And since that time she'd married Niles Westcott. A fact she'd very much like to forget.

"You always were a modest man, Quito," she said with a wicked little smile.

Rising to her feet, she gathered up her clothes, where he'd tossed them upon the grass, and quickly stepped into her jeans. By the time she was buttoning her blouse, Quito had also stood and was eyeing her with that quiet, Navajo way of his.

"What's the matter?" she asked.

"I was just thinking."

Forgetting the last button on her blouse, she closed the distance between them and slipped her arms around his waist. "I am a changed woman," she murmured gently. "The Clementine you just made love to would have never walked away from you eleven years ago."

He drew in a deep breath and let it out. "Is that supposed to make me feel better?"

Clementine didn't miss the faint bitterness twined through his words and her glance at him was tinged with sorrow. "That wasn't my reason for saying it," she tried to explain. "It was just something I wanted you to know."

"All right. So now I know it," he murmured.

But he didn't necessarily believe it, Clementine thought, as he eased her arms from around his waist. Well, it would be stupid of her to expect a few words from her lips to convince him. Besides, maybe in the long run it didn't matter whether he believed that she was a changed person. Even if Quito were to beg her, she couldn't stay here.

Clementine tried not to think about that dark fact as he reached for her hand and led her toward their waiting supper.

## Chapter Five

The next morning Clementine was about to leave her hotel room to have breakfast when the telephone beside her bed rang.

Tossing her handbag atop the tumbled covers, she picked up the shrilling instrument, wondering who would be calling her so early.

"Hello," she answered.

"Clementine! It's Victoria Ketchum. That is, Victoria Ketchum Hastings now," the woman added with a contented laugh. "I hope I'm not catching you at a bad time. I called early because I was afraid you'd be out later in the day."

A wide smile crossed Clementine's face. She'd never expected her old friend to call her. She'd been afraid Victoria had probably frowned upon her leaving Quito all those years ago and marked her off her list of friends. Apparently that hadn't been the case.

"How very nice to hear from you! How are you?" Clementine asked her.

Victoria laughed. "Busy. Happy. What about yourself?"

"I'm keeping busy, too." She wished she could truthfully add the happy part, too. But Clementine hadn't been happy for the past eleven years. There wasn't any use in trying to pretend otherwise.

"Are you wrapped up with anything this morning?" Victoria asked quickly. "I have about an hour before my patients start to arrive. I thought we might have coffee together and catch up."

"Actually I haven't even had breakfast yet," Clementine told her. "I was just about to get some when you called."

"Great! I was in too big of a rush to eat anything before I left the ranch. Let's meet at the Wagon Wheel and have one of those horribly fattening breakfasts," she suggested with a wicked laugh.

Heaven only knew how deep and dark Clementine's spirits were this morning. Just hearing Victoria's cheerful voice helped to lift her back into the sunlight.

"I'd love that. When should I be there?"

"Right now! I'm just a few blocks away. If you walk, we should be there at the same time."

"Walk?" Clementine questioned.

Victoria chuckled. "Yes, walking. It's good for you."

"Oh, yeah. Right, Doc," she replied with a laugh. "See you there."

Hanging up the phone, Clementine snatched up her handbag and hurried from the hotel. The morning was clear and already very warm. As she walked along the sidewalk, she didn't much notice the street traffic to her left or the landscaped businesses to her right. She was thinking back to the first time she'd met Victoria. Clementine's father had always made a point of attending the local political fund-raisers and that night she'd gone along with him. She had not expected to meet anyone even close to her own age, but Victoria had also been attending the function with her own father, Tucker.

Clementine's father had purchased horses from Tucker and the two men had become friendly. It was only normal that their two daughters should meet. And when Clementine was led over to a group of people, one of which was Victoria, her gaze stopped dead on the dark, tough sheriff standing near her elbow. Neil Rankin had also been with them, and he'd welcomed her into the little group with several jokes, mostly of which were directed at himself. Victoria had also been warm and friendly and Clementine had been drawn to her immediately. But it was Quito who'd made her pulse flutter and her cheeks burn with awareness.

At first he'd seemed not to notice her at all and had said very few words before their little group had broken up and scattered to other spots around the room. So she'd been surprised when, a few minutes later, he'd walked up and invited her to dance.

One waltz in Quito's arms and she'd been lost. It hadn't mattered that he'd said very little to her while they'd moved slowly around the dance floor. Something about the way his strong arms had held her, the way his dark brown eyes had looked into hers had shattered every thought, every dream she'd ever had of any man. That night he'd walked straight into her heart. And he'd never left.

With a soulful sigh, she tossed back her long blond hair and looked around to get her bearings. Across the street, on the corner was the Wagon Wheel diner. A tall, slender, dark-haired woman was standing near the entrance and Clementine knew instantly that the person was Victoria.

Picking up her pace, she jogged across the street and waved to Victoria as she drew near.

"You beat me," she called to her friend.

Victoria hurried down the sidewalk and flung her arms tightly around Clementine. "Clementine!

How wonderful to see you again," she said through happy tears.

Clementine pulled back just far enough to look at Victoria's beautiful face, then she hugged the woman again. "I'm so glad you called," she admitted, her eyes going misty. "I didn't know if you'd want to see me or not."

"Don't be silly," Victoria chided, then breaking their hug, she slipped her arm around Clementine's waist and urged her toward the diner's entrance. "Come on. We can talk better inside. And I need to order and eat before it's time to go back to the clinic."

Inside the diner, the two women made their way through the crowd until they found a booth that had just emptied. It was near a plate glass wall that overlooked Main street and as they took their seats Clementine thought how quiet and simple it would be to drive to work here in Aztec in the mornings. The cars and trucks lined up at the red light were seven or eight deep. But compared to the twelve lanes of traffic in Houston, this was nothing.

"How did you know I was here?" Clementine asked as they both settled themselves on the brown vinyl.

"Neil phoned me." Her eyes glowing, Victoria smiled at her. "It's so great to see you. And you look fabulous!"

Clementine smiled self-consciously at her friend's compliment. "Not really. But you—I can't believe you've had a baby! Your figure is still just as perfect as ever."

Victoria waved that notion away with the flip of her hand. "I'm hidden under this loose-fitting blouse."

Clementine started to speak, but a waitress suddenly arrived at their table. After the woman had taken their order and gone to fetch their coffee, she picked up the conversation where Victoria had left off.

"I can tell you're not hiding any baby fat," Clementine told her.

Still smiling, Victoria said, "I guess Neil told you about me getting married and having children."

Clementine nodded. "Uh-huh. He also told me about Ross and Seth getting married. Sounds like you Ketchums have really been walking down the aisle here lately."

"Yes. Isn't it wonderful? Finally I have children and sisters-in-law and hopefully I'll get some nieces and nephews soon."

Clementine smiled wanly. She couldn't help but be envious of Victoria's loving family. She'd been the only child of Wilfred and Delta. And as for a family of her very own, she'd pretty much shelved that idea once she'd discovered Niles's true character.

"I'm truly happy for you, Victoria. Although I was sorry to hear about your father passing. I know how close you two were."

Victoria's head bowed slightly and Clementine could see her friend was still feeling the grief of her father's death even though a few years had passed.

"Yes. We were close," she said huskily. "But in the end his health was really, really bad. He was on oxygen and in a wheelchair. To be honest, once he couldn't straddle a horse anymore, he wasn't the same man. It took all his will away." She looked across the table and smiled briefly at Clementine. "But let's not waste the morning talking about sad things. How long are you going to be in Aztec?"

Clementine spotted the waitress approaching with their coffee. She waited until their cups and saucers were settled and the woman walked away before she answered.

"I'm not sure." She shrugged as she stirred cream into the steaming coffee. "When I first decided to come up here, I'd planned on just a week's stay. But now I don't know. It may take more time than I thought to deal with the house."

Yeah, right, she thought with self-disgust. It wasn't the house that was on her mind. It was Quito. And the way he'd made love to her last night. Dear God, all she had to do was close her eyes and the fresh memories of being in his arms heated her whole body.

She didn't know what had come over her, why she'd urged the two of them to rekindle the fire that had once been between them. It wasn't like the two of them could ever have a life together. And making love to him was only going to make it harder for her to leave New Mexico.

Victoria finished a long sip of coffee as she studied her friend's face. "What about the house? Surely you're not thinking about selling it."

Clementine grimaced. "Actually I was. I don't have any need for it."

Victoria waved a dismissive hand at her. "What about vacations to be with your old friends up here in San Juan County?"

A wry smile touched Clementine's lips. "Well, I wasn't sure I had any friends up here."

"Oh, Clem. I don't know why you had such thoughts in your head. None of us was in any position to judge you back then. And we aren't now. You did what you thought was best. For yourself and for Quito."

"Yes." The word could barely get past her clogged throat. She tried to clear it with a little cough, then raised the coffee cup to her lips.

A few moments passed in silence as both women sipped their coffee. Eventually the waitress arrived with their meals. Bacon and eggs for Victoria. Sausage and pancakes for Clementine.

As the two of them started to eat, Victoria asked, "Speaking of Quito, have you seen him yet?"

Clementine drew in a bracing breath as she glanced across the table to her friend. "As a matter of fact, I've seen him three times. We had supper together last night."

Victoria's dark brows shot up. "Really? I'm surprised."

Clementine chuckled. "Well, this place is so small it would be impossible not to run into Quito. Especially with him being the sheriff. And we didn't part on nasty terms, after all."

Victoria slathered jam on a piece of toast. "No. You didn't. But Quito has been such a loner for so long. And we all know it's because of you. And—"

Before Victoria could say more, Clementine held up a hand asking her to put on the brakes.

"Victoria, that's all in the past. If you think Quito has been carrying a torch for me, then you're wrong. We're just old friends. That's all we can be now."

A frown of concern wrinkled Victoria's forehead. "Oh, Clementine, forgive me if I assumed too much. But I've always had this feeling that Quito hasn't gotten over you."

"Oh." She swallowed at the knot in her throat and forced a bite of pancakes into her mouth.

"But I suppose after all this time that probably doesn't matter to you," Victoria added.

Clementine's head jerked up with surprise and her eyes locked on with Victoria's. "That's a caustic thing to say!"

"Well, it doesn't matter, does it? You just insisted

the two of you were only friends. And besides," she added with a sly smile, "I'm sure you're married now. With children, I hope."

Shaking her head, Clementine looked down at her plate. "I'm divorced, Victoria, and have been for more than two years. We didn't have any children."

"Oh. I'm sorry."

She let out a heavy breath. "Me, too," she said, then added, "what do you know about the shooting that wounded Quito? I can't imagine anyone around here that would do such a thing. When we lived here, everyone seemed to admire and respect him. But I suppose a sheriff does make some enemies over the years."

"I probably don't know much more than he told you," Victoria said with a frown. "Jess doesn't usually give me any inside information. Department policy and all that."

"Well, Quito didn't tell me much, either. Except that someone drove up beside his vehicle and shot him." She looked candidly across the table to Victoria. "What do you think? Do you have any idea who it might have been or why?"

Slipping a bite of egg into her mouth, Victoria shook her head glumly. After she swallowed, she said, "There are no leads for the detectives to go on. Other than someone spotted a Dodge pickup with dark windows somewhere in the vicinity of the shooting. It had Nevada plates, but the person didn't catch any of the numbers. And even that clue might not be pertinent to the shooting. Could have just been some innocent person driving down the highway."

"That's the only clue they have?" Clementine asked with disbelief. "Surely they have something else!"

Once again Victoria shook her head. "Since the shooter was inside a truck, there weren't even any shell casings to be found."

The hope of finding whoever committed the heinous crime appeared to be slim to none, Clementine thought uneasily. "That's scary, Victoria. This killer—or maniac—whatever he is…might try to kill Quito again! Do you think he's watching out for himself?"

Last night, during the time Clementine had spent with him, she hadn't noticed him taking any sort of extra precautions for his safety. As far as she could recall, he hadn't even once looked over his shoulder. But then Quito had never been one to fear for himself. Only others.

Victoria's expression was sympathetic. "I don't think so. You know Quito. He doesn't ever worry about his own hide. He just wants to make sure everyone else in the county is safe."

.Clementine nodded and focused her attention on the pancakes on her plate. Normally she loved the sinfully sweet breakfast, but this morning she might as well have been chewing tree bark soaked in syrup. Her mind, her whole body was consumed with Quito.

Making love to him had shaken her deeply, even more deeply than it had eleven years ago. And maybe that was because she was a mature woman now and she appreciated all the things that she'd lost.

"So what are you doing with yourself now, Clementine?"

Relieved to focus on something else besides Quito, Clementine looked up. "I'm doing relief work. You know, overseas with needy children and adults. I just got back from Afghanistan about a week ago."

Victoria's eyes were suddenly glowing with interest. "How exciting. Gosh, you'll have to tell me all about it. Do you have any pictures with you?"

"A few. Back with my things in the hotel."

Victoria thoughtfully tapped her fork against the side of her plate. "And speaking of hotels. We've got to do something about you staying there. It's just awful to think you're paying for a room, when I'd love to have you stay out at the ranch. So would my husband. He loves having beautiful women around," she joked.

"Oh, no. I couldn't impose. You have children and a husband and a job. You don't have time to entertain a guest. Or have another body underfoot."

Victoria chuckled. "Who said anything about you being a guest? I'd probably put you to work cleaning the kitchen or cooking."

To know that Victoria still treasured their friendship filled her with happy relief and she laughed along with her. "That wouldn't be a problem. I've learned to wash dishes out of a galvanized wash pan." Reaching across the table, she touched Victoria's hand. "Thank you for asking me. I'll think about it. Okay?"

"Think hard. And in the meantime, don't do anything with the Jones house. It's so beautiful and I know that someday you'll be glad you have it."

Smiling wanly, Clementine said, "Maybe I won't do anything in a hurry about the house. Who knows," she added with a shrug, "I might even decide to clean it up and stay a few days longer."

At the same time Clementine and Victoria were finishing their breakfast, a grim-faced Jess was pacing around Quito's office.

"I don't like this, Quito. And I don't believe it's a joke, either."

Quito glanced down at the small square of paper lying in front of him. It was a short message, written in carefully printed letters. *Next time I'll get the job done.*

Of course the envelope had no return address on the front or back. The only apparent clue was the Las Vegas postage stamp.

"This proves that the truck with the Nevada plates belonged to the shooter! This also proves that someone is going to try to kill you again. And this time they might just succeed!"

Quito stifled a heavy sigh. He wasn't exactly

pleased to find a death threat waiting for him in his morning mail. But then he shouldn't have been surprised to find it. Clearly the person who'd shot him had been aiming to kill. And after going to such lengths to try to blow him away, it was pretty obvious the person wouldn't stop until the job was done.

"I can't run and hide in the closet," Quito growled. Then frowning, he looked up at his under sheriff. "Go get a plastic bag from forensics and we'll send this thing to the lab down at Albuquerque. If we're lucky they'll find prints or DNA mixed in with the glue on the back of the envelope. I can't tell, but it looks as though the stamp was a self-adhesive kind."

Jess started out the door to follow Quito's order, then paused to look back at him. "Quito, I know this is a silly question, but do you know anyone in Las Vegas? Someone you angered or arrested?"

Releasing a dismal sigh, Quito shook his head. "No. Not at all. But that doesn't surprise me. I figure this is a gun for hire."

Surprise crossed Jess's features. "You think someone was hired to kill you?"

Leaning back in his leather chair, Quito wearily pinched the bridge of his nose. He wasn't in the mood to talk about someone killing him. Clementine was already doing a good job of that. Just give her a little more time and the Nevada thug wouldn't have to make another try. His heart would already have holes in it.

"Sure do. Why? You hadn't thought of that notion?"

With a frown, Jess swung his head back and forth. "Actually I hadn't. It seemed like an angry crime—not like a cold assassination from afar."

Quito shrugged. "You might be right. But I don't think so. It's just a feeling I have more than anything."

Both men suddenly looked toward the door as whistling out in the hallway grew closer and closer to Quito's office door.

"Who the hell?" Quito started to rise from his chair at the same time Neil Rankin rounded the door facing. There was a wide grin on his face and he looked so damn cheerful Quito wanted to shout at him.

"Good mornin' guys. Am I interrupting? Julie gave me permission to come on back."

Quito grunted. "Remind me to dock Julie's paycheck," he joked with a heavy growl. "And it wouldn't matter to you if you were interrupting, Neil. You'd come into my office anyway."

"So," Neil said as he strode straight to Quito's coffeepot. "You'd do the same if it were my office."

Quito couldn't argue with that. Over the years there had been many times he'd burst in on Neil and interrupted his workday. But good friends could do that to each other and get away with it. And Neil had become his good friend even before Quito had become sheriff fifteen years ago.

"I'll leave you two to fight it out," Jess said and quickly exited the room.

Neil finished pouring a cup full of coffee and carried it over to a chair sitting at an angle to Quito's desk. He sat down, crossed his ankles and sipped his coffee under Quito's squinted gaze.

"What are you doing here this morning? Don't you have work to do?"

"Later. One client was late, then called to say she couldn't make it at all. Must have broken a fingernail or something."

Quito rolled his eyes. "God help you if you're representing a woman that ditzy."

"I'd represent anyone for the right kind of money," Neil said glibly.

Quito scowled at him. "That's a bald-faced lie and we both know it. You do have principles."

Neil chuckled. "Yeah. At least I don't chase ambulances."

"What are you doing here? Just killing time and wasting mine?"

Neil cleared his throat and leveled a pointed look on Quito. "Actually I'm being nosy. I wanted to know how your dinner with Clementine went last night."

His eyes suddenly wide, Quito stared at him. "How did you know about that?"

Chuckling again, Neil said, "Great day, Quito! You know nothing stays quiet in this town. The news that your old flame is back in town has raced down the streets like floodwater from a broken dam. I'm surprised the phone lines aren't jammed."

Quito opened his mouth to make a retort, but Jess chose that moment to reappear with the plastic bag.

He knocked on the door facing. "If you'll let me get that thing, I'll be out of your hair," he told Quito.

Quito motioned for him to come on and finish his business. Neil's expression suddenly perked up as Jess leaned over the desk.

"Get what thing? What sort of thing?"

"None of your business," Quito snapped.

With a pair of tweezers, Jess picked up the envelope and the accompanying piece of paper. As he dropped it into a plastic bag with a zip lock closure, Neil said, "Quito, you know I always keep my lips super-glued. Come on and let me in on this lab study."

"I'll ship it off right now. Or would you rather one of the deputies drive it down to Albuquerque?" Jess asked.

"Drive it," Quito said without hesitation. "I want to make damn sure the thing isn't lost or tampered with. And tell whoever takes it he'd better not be monkeying around on the way down there."

"Will do."

Jess started out of the room. "Nice to see you, Neil. Why don't you come out and see us sometime? We'll saddle up Pokie and Star and cut a few calves."

Neil laughed. "Lord, I haven't been on a horse in months, Jess. And cutting—hell, that would kill me. But thanks for asking. I'll think about it."

Nodding, Jess went on out the door. Behind him, Quito yelled, "Shut that door. And tell Julie not to send a soul back here. Even if they're confessing to murder."

"I'll handle them," Jess assured him, then firmly shut the door on the two men.

Neil scooted up to the edge of the hard wooden seat and looked at Quito with a condescending eye. "All right. Jess is gone. Tell me what that letter was that he carried out in a plastic bag. Evidence on what or who?"

Quito didn't normally let any sort of information leak from his department. But he was certain Neil would never open his mouth. And if he didn't tell his friend, he would keep hounding him till Quito would get the urge to box his jaws.

Rising from his chair, Quito walked over to the coffeepot and poured himself a cup of the tarry brew. Even though it was still fairly early in the morning, he'd been here since six and so had the coffee. "It wasn't a letter. It was a message—one line."

"To you?"

Quito shrugged. "It appears that way. The envelope was addressed to me."

"What did it say?"

"I shouldn't tell you. It wouldn't do a bit of good if I did."

"Tell me anyway," Neil ordered.

His friend's expression had gone grim in the past few moments and Quito understood that ever since the shooting, Neil had been worried about him. He and Daniel Redwing had taken turns sitting up with Quito at the hospital. Although at the time Quito had been unconscious and wouldn't have known if Dr. Kildaire himself had been in the room. Still it touched him deep down to know that the two men hadn't left him to die alone.

"It's not that big a deal, Neil. Just a little death threat. It might even be someone playing a prank," he said, trying to play the whole thing down.

Neil snorted. "I doubt that. Just go look at the bloodstains in your vehicle."

"They're not in there anymore. Since it was my work vehicle, the department paid for new seats and carpet."

Neil rolled his eyes with worried frustration. "I'm glad about that. But me and you both know that if someone sent you a death threat, it's probably from the person who tried to kill you a month ago."

Sighing heavily, Quito leaned his head against the back of his chair. "Yeah. Probably. Most likely. And when you think about it, that note might be an answer to my prayers. We desperately need a lead in this case, Neil. Otherwise, I might never know who wants me dead."

Grimacing, Neil leaned up and placed his cup on the edge of Quito's desk. "Well, I wish all of this wasn't happening now," he said, then shook his head, "Hell, I wish it wasn't happening at any time. But with Clementine here I wanted things to be happy for both of you."

His eyes narrow, Quito leaned forward to stare at his friend. "Happy? How could anything ever be happy for me and Clementine?"

"Well, they sure as hell can't be with someone shooting at you," Neil quipped.

Quito cursed under his breath. "Neil, wake up. If you've got some far-fetched idea that Clementine came back to resume our relationship, then you're in some sort of medicated fog. Or you've been having too many beers down at Indian Wells."

"I don't take medication and I had one beer last night. That's not enough alcohol to fog a brain like mine," he joked wryly. "You're the one who needs to wake up. Clementine is still crazy about you. All I had to do is mention your name and I could see it all over her face."

Quito's heart winced with bittersweet pain. He wasn't going to try to deny that Clementine still felt something for him. But it wasn't love. She was addicted to his sex, that was all. And he couldn't be a fool and let himself think the way she'd clung to him last night was anything but physical need.

"Like I said, you're seeing things through a fog. You'd better ease up on your work schedule."

Neil cursed. "Okay. You tell me, Quito. What happened last night? Did you two enjoy each other's company?"

Damn it, Quito thought, as he felt hot color creep up his neck and into his face, it shouldn't bother him to talk about Clementine. But that was hard to do when memories of last night were eating him up inside. "Of course; we did. We're not juveniles, cutting each other down for what happened in the past. Clementine is a special woman to me."

"Tell me something I don't already know. Where did you go to eat? Over to Farmington to some fancy place with dim lighting and low music?" Neil asked with a suggestive wiggle of his eyebrows.

"That's really none of your business. But—" He shrugged one shoulder as if conceding to his friend. "Clem wanted to go on a picnic, so that's what we did. Fried chicken, the whole lot."

Quito expected Neil to burst out laughing but instead he leveled a serious look on him as he said, "Look, Quito, a lot of men don't get a second chance in life. You've just been given two. Don't waste them, buddy."

Quito's gaze slipped from Neil's face to latch on

to the distant mountains framed by the windows across the room. Neil didn't have to tell him what two chances he was talking about. One was cheating death by surviving his bullet wounds. The other was having Clementine back in town.

Maybe he should be feeling lucky and good about the future. But all he could think about was the day Clementine would be leaving again.

## *Chapter Six*

Later that morning, Clementine sat in her hotel room, staring out the window as she waited for an answer on the other end of her cell phone. She was calling a family friend, Oscar Ramirez, a lawyer who oversaw her father's business dealings and also tended to anything legal that the Jones family needed.

During her divorce, Oscar had made sure she contemplated everything with a level head, instead of her emotions. Which had been a lifesaver considering she wanted to buy a gun and go after Niles. Now she was happy she hadn't killed him. Life wouldn't be much fun living inside a prison cell. And life right now felt downright wonderful.

"Oscar here."

Clementine jerked her thoughts off the flowers and the meadow and Quito's strong arms around her.

"Oscar. It's Clem. How are things going? Do you have time to talk a minute?"

"For you, all the time you need, Clem," he said. "And as for things here, they're going good. I heard from your parents yesterday. They were in Greece for a little two-day tour. Will didn't sound all that enthused but he says Delta is having a blast."

"Daddy would rather be in south Texas hunting white-tailed deer," Clementine said with a little laugh, then asked, "nothing else has happened down there? You haven't had any calls asking about me, have you?"

Oscar didn't have to be told that she was talking about Niles and Clementine's spirits fell flat as Oscar deliberately cleared his throat. "Sorry to tell you this, Clem, but I had a visit here at the office rather than a call."

Jumping to her feet, Clementine gripped the phone. "Niles came to your office? Dear God, Oscar, what did he want?"

The lawyer let out a long breath. "The usual. He threw around a lot of threats. Said he'd do bodily harm to me if I didn't tell him where you were."

"Did you?"

"Of course not! The man would have to kill me first, Clem. I don't want that monster around you any more than your parents do. And they're depending on me to keep you safe. Although, I don't really know how I'm supposed to do that with you up there in New Mexico."

Her shoulders sagged as a fatalistic weight suddenly dropped upon her. "Oscar, don't be worrying about me. I won't have you hurt just because of me. It's not your fault that I married a man that turned into a monster. How did you get rid of him?"

"My secretary had enough good sense to call security after he barged into my office. Niles was just getting wound up good when they came in and carted him away. He was flinging a few curse words over his shoulder at me when they strong-armed him out of here."

Clementine let out a heavy sigh. "I'm so sorry, Oscar. I just don't know what to do anymore."

"Hon, you've already tried everything you could think of. Short of killing the man, the best thing you can do is stay away from Houston. If he catches wind of where you are, well, I don't have to tell you what will happen."

Squeezing her eyes shut, Clementine pinched the bridge of her nose and tried her best to keep anger and weariness from overtaking her. "No. I've already been through it too many times before. Only this time, if he came up here...I'm not sure what would happen. Let's just say the county sheriff is a modern-day Wyatt Earp."

Oscar's chuckles were far more cunning than humorous. "Hmm. Maybe that's exactly what Niles needs—to face a tough cowboy with a gun on his hip."

No! Dear God no, Clementine thought desperately. She didn't care what happened to Niles, but she wasn't about to chance Quito's safety. He'd nearly lost his life once. And if Niles should ever learn that she and Quito were once lovers, he would no doubt try to kill him. Niles was a psychopath. It wouldn't take much to push him to commit murder. For as long as she lived, Clementine would never forget the blows of his fists upon her face. Yet in his sick mind, he believed he'd been doing it out of love.

Shuddering at the dark thought, Clementine said, "Oscar, if he corners you again, just lie. Send him to the East Coast, or anywhere, except here."

"Got it, hon. So now that we have that out of the way, how are things going up there? Do you have things settled with a real estate agent yet?"

Moving closer to the window, Clementine looked down upon the rooftops spanned out over the high desert town. Two blocks over, Quito was probably sitting at his desk, going over arrest warrants, or discussing a case with his chief deputy. Had she entered his mind this morning? she wondered. Heaven help her, he was all she could think about.

"Uh, no," she answered Oscar's question. "Not yet. I'm still trying to decide what to do with the place."

"What do you mean? You told me you were going to sell it."

Clementine grimaced. She was losing her focus, she thought. She'd come up here to New Mexico with a purpose, but one look at Quito and her senses had spun out in all sorts of crazy directions. "I know I did. But I'm beginning to wonder if that's the right thing to do. I really love it up here. I have old friends around the county. And the house would make a nice getaway for me. I always was partial to the place."

The line went silent for a few moments and she realized Oscar was contemplating everything she'd just told him. That was always one of the things she liked about him the most. He thought before he spoke.

"Well," he finally said. "That's for you to decide. And I'm certainly not going to urge you to come back to Houston. Not as long as Niles is breathing."

It wasn't like Oscar to be talking so tough and the corners of her lips tilted upward as she thought about Quito and how he would describe her father's lawyer. Milksop. Dapper dandy. But he was fiercely loyal and he loved the Jones family as much as he did his own.

"I'm going to drive out to the house this morning and see if I can do a bit of cleaning," she told him. "I think I might have the utilities turned on and stay a few days. The weather is much nicer here than in

Houston right now. And with Mother and Daddy away, there's not much reason for me to be there."

"Sounds all right to me, Clem. But I really wish you'd let me send a bodyguard up there for you. For some reason, I have this feeling that something is about to happen." He chuckled as though he realized his words might upset her and he needed to soften them. "Maybe I should just read my horoscope and check the stock market. The past few days crude oil has been spiking. Delta will be glad to hear Wilfred can buy her another new Cadillac for Christmas."

Clementine chuckled. "It'll probably be diamonds this year. Or a ski trip to Telluride. So many stars have homes there she thinks she'll get a glimpse of one."

Oscar laughed outright and then the two of them began to wind down the conversation. By the time Clementine said goodbye and hung up the phone, she felt a bit better.

After all, she told herself, as she picked up her handbag and headed out of the hotel room, she'd dealt with Niles's threats for three years now. There wasn't any point in letting him get her spirits down now.

But things were different now, she argued with herself. She was back in Aztec. And for a few minutes last night, she'd been back in Quito's arms. A place where she'd often prayed to be. And this morning when her eyes had first fluttered open, she'd actually felt a spurt of happiness, she'd even had a glimmer of hope that her life was finally going to head in the right direction.

Niles could do more than hurt her physically now. He could ruin everything. And no matter what, she couldn't allow that to happen.

One day was all Quito could stand before he had to go looking for Clementine. He'd expected her to drop by the sheriff's department yesterday and maybe even invite him on another picnic, or at least to dinner at the diner. But she hadn't appeared and he'd gone home feeling a little hurt and cross with himself. Which was stupid really. Just because he'd had sex with a woman didn't mean she would start falling all over him and begging for more.

Now he was headed for the Jones house. It was the last place he could think of where to look. Unless she'd decided to run back to Texas, he thought, grimly.

Minutes later he found Clementine's dark sports car parked beneath the stone steps leading up to the yard surrounding the big house. He parked his own vehicle next to hers and started the steep climb up to the yard. Once he'd reached the porch, he could see the windows to the house were all raised and the front door was standing wide-open. He could hear the muted tones of music coming from one of the rooms and the sound of Clementine's melodious voice singing along.

He paused on the threshold and simply listened. For years he'd thought of her voice, hungered to hear its sweetness, and now it washed through him like warm rain on a dusty day.

Enough moments passed for him to begin to feel foolish, so he lifted his fist and rapped on the door facing.

"Clementine? You have company." He walked through the large foyer and stood at the edge of the living room.

The singing suddenly stopped and he caught the rapid sound of her footsteps coming from the wing of bedrooms.

A few seconds later, she appeared, hurrying toward him with a smile on her face that made his heart flutter like a damn teenager. He'd always believed that once a man got past a certain age, he'd lose all those strong reactions to the female gender. And for the most part, he had lost them. For the past few years women hadn't held that much of an interest for him. Thanks to Clementine. But now that she was back, his libido seemed to be coming to vivid life again.

"Quito! What are you doing here?"

One corner of his mouth lifted. "Searching for a missing person."

Concern crossed her face and then her mouth formed an *O*. "You mean me?"

"You're the only person I haven't been able to lo-cate," he said.

Laughing softly, she began to brush dust from the thighs of her jeans. "I've been busy. Besides, I didn't figure you wanted me pestering you."

She was a pest all right, he thought, but in the sweetest kind of way. "I thought you might have gone back to Texas."

Surprise jerked her head up and her blue eyes scanned his face. "Without telling you goodbye? Quito, you know me better than that."

Did he? All he knew that deep down, he'd some-how known she would return to him someday. What he didn't know was just exactly how long she would stay. And that question was already tearing at his heart, consuming his thoughts.

"Well, it's not like we've communicated all these years."

The slant of her smile was full of regrets. "No. But we've—uh, communicated since I've been here."

That was an understatement, Quito thought. The information her body had sent him the night of their picnic had been frank and fiery. So much so that the memory of it still caused a flame to burn low in his belly.

"Yeah," he mumbled, then forced himself to look away from her and glance around the room. The dust covers had been taken down from the furniture and the oak floor was shining. The drapes and blinds had been removed from the windows, allowing streams of evening sunshine to slant across the polished floor.

"What have you been doing? Cleaning?"

She laughed at the skeptical note in his voice. "Why, yes, Quito. In spite of what you think, I do know how to handle a mop and broom. I've even learned how to use a scrub brush," she said with exaggerated pride.

He looked back at her, his lips flattened with a tight grimace. "That's not what I meant. Why are you cleaning? I thought you were putting this place up for sale."

She moved forward, bringing her body within inches of his. Quito instantly felt himself reacting to her feminine scent and the tanned bare shoulders exposed by the gypsy blouse riding on the curves of her upper arms.

He drew in a deep breath and released it while he wondered how he was going to keep his hands off her or if he should even try.

"I haven't made up my mind yet," she said simply.

His brows drew together. "Isn't that why you came up here?"

It was the excuse she'd given herself, Clementine thought. But the more she thought about her motives, the more she realized she'd wanted any reason to see Quito. For years, she'd done her best to put him out of her mind. She'd done her best to make a life apart from his. It hadn't worked. And though she didn't expect Quito to pick up where they'd left off, she needed this time with him to heal. To look back on all her mistakes and forgive herself for making them.

Feeling unexpectedly shy, her gaze fell to their feet. "At first the house was my sole reason for driving up here. But then I saw you in the diner." Lifting her eyes back to his face, she smiled in a bittersweet way. "You always were impossible for me to resist."

Knowing he was being seduced without her even trying, Quito breathed deeply once again and stepped around her. "The place is beginning to shape up. How long have you been working on it?"

"I started yesterday. It's hard to do anything without electricity. But the power company promised they'd be out tomorrow to turn it on. In the meantime, I've done what I could with just a broom and a mop. Want to look at the other rooms?"

The last thing he needed to do was take a waltz with her through several bedrooms. Especially if she'd stripped the dust covers off the mattresses. He probably wouldn't be able to stop himself from tossing her onto the bed and making love to her until neither one of them could move or talk. But he was a smart enough man to know that the more he made love to her, the more he would want to.

"No. Maybe later. I really need to get home."

Disappointment drooped the corners of her mouth. "Oh."

That one simple word from her lips was enough to make him feel awful. Why was it, he wondered, that to make Clementine smile was enough to fill his own soul with sunshine?

"But I thought you might like to go with me and have supper. I'll cook you an Angus steak. Rib eye or T-bone. Your choice."

The invitation both surprised and pleased her and she was suddenly smiling widely. "Really? Well, I'm going to hold you to that, Quito Perez. I want to see if your New Mexico beef is as good as ours down in Texas."

She quickly glanced down at herself. "But I'm so nasty. Maybe I should clean myself up first."

Shaking his head, Quito slipped his arm around her bare shoulders. "Forget that. You look beautiful. Even with dust on your nose. And no one is going to see you but me."

Chuckling happily, she slid her arm against the back of his waist. "What a liar you are," she murmured.

At the door Clementine paused long enough to lock it and then the two of them made the climb down the hill to where their vehicles sat parked together.

As Clementine started to climb into hers, Quito said, "Don't bother with taking your car. I'll bring you back."

With her hand on the door handle, she arched a brow at him. "Are you sure? That's a lot of bother."

He made a scoffing noise. "The ranch is only about five miles away. We'll be there in no time."

Clementine had never been inside a law enforcement cruiser before and at first she was a little taken aback by all the paraphernalia attached to the dashboard and nestled on the floorboard between the seats.

The two-way radio crackled with static even before Quito started the engine and as he maneuvered the SUV around the sound of a female dispatcher could be heard talking to a deputy about a truck that had been abandoned on a dirt road.

As soon as Quito had the vehicle moving forward he reached over and shut off the sound of the communication device. "Sorry about that," he said.

Half grinning, she said, "I'm really not supposed to be riding with you, am I? This is a government work vehicle."

He sent her an amused look. "I'm working. I just found my lost person. Now I'm taking her to a safe place of shelter. I'm not breaking any law."

Smiling, she snuggled back in the seat. It was so nice to feel like a damsel being saved by a dark knight. Quito had always made her feel that way. Safe, loved, protected. She'd been crazy to leave all those years ago. She knew that with certainty now and had known it for quite some time. But the past couldn't be changed. And at the time, she'd been very young and very insecure. Especially where a man like Quito was concerned. He'd been too masculine, too sexy, too everything for her to handle with confidence. She'd been so afraid of marrying him, then failing as a wife and messing up both their lives. Yet it seemed as though she'd done that anyway.

The last of her thoughts she pushed away as best she could and tried to focus on the night to come. Fretting about the past would only ruin the present. And she had to make the most of her time here with Quito. Because she knew the sand was quickly running out of her hourglass.

Quito still lived in the same house his adoptive parents had owned throughout their lives. It was one of the few houses in the area that was made of rock and Quito could recite the stories his father often told about how he'd gone all the way to Creed, Colorado, and loaded the rocks without the help of anyone. His father had so many flat tires on his truck it had taken him three days to get back to San Juan County. But once the masonry was finished on the house, he'd been so pleased with the beauty, he'd forgotten all about the misery of the trip.

"Why, Quito, I see cows and horses. Do they belong to you or have you leased the pasture?" Clementine asked as they neared the Perez family home place.

"They're mine. I didn't have enough to keep me busy," he said jokingly. "So I decided to start running a few livestock on the ranch again. Dad would have wanted it."

He stopped the vehicle in front of a wooden fence, most of which was covered with some sort of green vine. To Clementine, the house looked unchanged. The round, multicolored rocks were a little more weathered but the gables were still painted a rustic brown. The trees and bushes dressing the yard had grown taller, but other than that, she felt as if she were stepping back in time as she waited for him to help her down from the truck.

"It looks beautiful, Quito," she said as she draped her hand in his and gracefully touched her toes to the ground. "You must work very hard to keep everything looking so well maintained. Your father would be proud."

"I like to think so," he told her.

He shut the vehicle door, then took her by the upper arm. As he gently guided her toward the front of the house, she said, "Neil told me that you lost them both in a short amount of time. I'm so sorry. I know how much you loved them."

He released her arm and opened a heavy wooden door with a horseshoe for a knocker. "I was their chosen one. No one can imagine the love I felt for them."

Clementine understood what he was trying to tell her. Quito's real parents were basically unknown. His mother had been a Navajo teenager who'd run away from the reservation at the age of fourteen. Some had said she'd craved the excitement of the white man's cities, but others had told Quito's adoptive parents that her father had abused her and she'd had no choice but to flee the reservation to save herself.

In either case, the young woman had wound up homeless and pregnant by a man she wouldn't identify. Eventually the teen had been forced to return to Gallup for help and she'd delivered Quito in a medicine woman's wickiup. Three days later, she disappeared without a trace and Quito was taken to a foster home.

Clementine always found herself close to tears when she thought about Quito's birth and upbringing. He was such a handsome, intelligent, compassionate man it was hard to believe that as a baby he'd been handed from one home to another until the Perez family had eventually taken him in and made him their legal son.

"You were lucky to have them, Quito," she said. "Were either of them ill for very long?"

He ushered her into the house before he answered.

"Dad's heart condition went on for several years. But once he died, Mom just lost her will to fight her diabetes. I think she just couldn't bear to be without him. They'd been married for sixty-five years. Always at each other's side. It was meant for them to go together."

The only response Clementine could give him

was a slight nod of her head. She was too busy imagining her and Quito together, year after year until they were old and frail. With Quito by her side, aging wouldn't be something to dread. Together they could truly have golden years.

"Clem? Are you with me?"

She blinked as she realized Quito was speaking to her and she'd been staring off into space.

"Oh, sorry, Quito. I was thinking—"

"Obviously," he said wryly.

A sad little smile quirked her lips. "I was thinking how lucky your parents were to have had all those years together. Some people go through life never finding a mate."

"Yeah," he said a bit gruffly. "And then some people find them and then lose them." His face stoic, he urged her forward. "I'm getting hungry. If you'd like to freshen up, I'll fix us something to drink. What would you like?"

"Anything that you're having will be fine with me," she told him. "Is the bathroom still in the same place?"

He inclined his head toward an arched doorway leading down a long, dark hallway. "Still there. I'll be in the kitchen."

She watched him walk out of the room and then she took a moment to allow her curious gaze to roam around her surroundings.

Surprisingly the house didn't look that different on the inside, either. There were a few pieces of furniture and the window treatments were new to Clementine. The tile floor was still the same, though, as were the plastered walls which were covered with the same family photos and stuffed game.

Back when she'd lived in town, she'd spent a lot of time in this house with Quito and his family. They had been very nice to her and she'd grown to love them even though she'd gotten the feeling they didn't entirely approve of her. They'd feared that Clementine would hurt their son. At least that's what Quito had confided in her. And ironically, she supposed their fears had turned true. She'd run from Quito and this life like a scared chicken.

With a silent groan of self-disgust, she turned on her heel and hurried through the dark to the bathroom. It was too late to lament about the past, she furiously told herself. *Think about tonight. Think how blessed you are to have these hours with him.*

A few minutes later she found her way to the kitchen where she found Quito adding ice to two margaritas.

"Oh. We're having something alcoholic?" she asked with surprise.

He handed her one of the drinks. "What's the matter? You don't drink alcohol?"

"On a special occasion I do." And this was very

special, she thought, as she raised the glass to her lips. "Mmm. You even salted the rim of the glass."

"Nothing's too good for a Texas heiress."

She pursed her lips at him. "Don't call me that."

He chuckled. "I thought all you Texans were proud of your heritage."

"I'm not talking about the Texas part. It's the heiress word I don't cotton to."

He swallowed some of his drink, then placed the glass onto the cabinet counter. "You can't deny what you are. Your parents are filthy rich and someday you'll inherit it all."

She edged toward him. "That's true. But that's not what I'm all about."

From the corner of his eye, he caught her gaze. "Really? Then why did you leave all those years ago?"

She began to tremble inside as she watched him reach for his glass and then down half the strong mixture of tequila. No sound of accusation or bitterness had been threaded through his words, yet she knew that deep down he must harbor some of those feelings toward her. And if she ever accomplished anything in her life, she wanted to take all that away. She wanted the only man in her life to view her in the best of ways.

"You really want to know?" she asked quietly.

One dark eyebrow quirked upward as he studied her face. "You mean you've come up with something other than being too young and spoiled?"

She sipped a bit of the margarita in hopes the alcohol would smooth the frazzled nerves jumping throughout her body.

"That much was the truth. Along with the fact that I was scared to death," she admitted.

He studied her for long moments, then with a scoffing snort, he turned to a package of meat lying on the cabinet counter. As he unwrapped the white freezer paper, he said, "Clementine Jones wasn't scared of anything back then. And I doubt you're scared of anything now. Anyone that travels to war-torn countries as you have can't have a weak constitution."

He couldn't begin to imagine the fear she'd lived through the past few years, Clementine thought. But she didn't want him to know about that. She didn't want his pity. And she didn't want him getting involved in something that might cause him danger. The less he knew about Niles the better.

"Well, I'm a little more grown up now. Or can't you tell?" she asked, her cheeks dimpled impishly.

He glanced over at her and a smile briefly touched his lips. "You look like the same beautiful, seductive woman to me."

"Maybe with a few more wrinkles," she said wryly. "But I like to think I've gained a bit more wisdom, Quito. And when I think back to—when I was here—with you, I realize how little I knew about love and marriage. At the time, I had enough sense to know that I was spoiled. That in all my young years I'd never had to care for myself. It was pretty clear I didn't have the ability to take care of a husband. I needed to do some growing up in the worst kind of way."

His hands paused in their task, but he didn't look at her as he spoke. "I would have given you time. I would have waited," he said thickly.

Tears were suddenly burning her eyes and she moved close enough to wrap her hand around his forearm. The moment she touched him, he turned to look at her.

"I didn't know, Quito. I thought I was doing what was best for both of us. But once I was back in Houston and the days turned into months, I realized I was miserable without you."

"Why didn't you contact me? Why didn't you come back?"

The pain eating at her heart forced her gaze to tear away from his. "Because I thought you'd probably found someone else. And even if you hadn't found someone else, you probably wouldn't have forgiven me." She sighed and rubbed her burning eyelids with the pads of her fingertips. "So I stayed in Houston, finished my college education and convinced myself that marrying a man of my own means would be best—that I'd be doing the right thing. Dear God, what a mistake that was. Niles was a bastard. That's the only way to describe him."

Slipping her left hand up his arm, she rested the right one in the middle of his broad chest. "What about you, Quito? You didn't find a woman you wanted to marry?"

A groan sounded deep in his throat. "Clementine, since you left I've been worthless to women." With his hands on her shoulders, he tugged her up against him and buried his face in the side of her long, silken hair.

Clementine wrapped her arms around his waist and clung tightly. "Let's forget supper," she whispered urgently. "I can't eat now. I want you too much."

## Chapter Seven

Quito couldn't argue. Not when Clementine was saying everything he was feeling.

Lifting his head, he tilted her face up to his and took her lips in a devouring kiss that lasted so long his body turned hard and hungry.

"I think we'd better go to the bedroom," he whispered huskily. "Unless you want to test the sturdiness of the kitchen table."

Her arms circled his neck as her senses continued to swirl madly. He hadn't just kissed her. His lips had made love to hers. And now the rest of her body was aching for him.

"I don't care," she said with a breathless rush. "Anywhere. Just make love to me, Quito."

Instantly he bent down and scooped her up in his arms. As he started across the room with her, she expected him to deposit her on the long pine table positioned near the windows. But instead he carried her out of the room and down the long hallway.

Eventually they passed through an open doorway to the left and the next thing she knew he was placing her in the middle of a queen-size-bed.

Since the sun had already set for the day, the room was bathed in shadows, but still had enough light for her to see a matching dresser and chest, a straight back chair piled with clothing and a wooden hall-tree loaded down with all types of cowboy hats.

"Is this where you sleep?" she asked as he lay down next to her.

"When I'm fortunate enough to sleep," he said.

He reached for her and she rolled toward him, her hand coming to rest on his healing ribs. "The shooting still haunts you, I'm sure."

"I try not to think about it. But my subconscious takes over the moment I go to sleep. In my dreams I feel the slice of the bullets, the fiery pain and I'm cursing because I can't get out of the vehicle and go after the bastard who did it."

She swallowed at the thick emotions clogging her

throat. "Maybe once you find him, your nightmares will stop."

"Maybe having you here like this will stop them," he murmured as he dragged her closer against his body.

Her mouth searched for his and in a matter of seconds their lips were desperately grinding against each other, their tongues entwined, their fingers locked as he brought her arms above her head and turned her onto her back.

With his body covering hers, he teased her with kiss after kiss until finally his lips broke away from her and began a long, sensual descent down her neck and onto her shoulder.

As his lips worked their magic on her senses, Clementine began to release the buttons down the front of his shirt. Her fingers moved swiftly until the fabric parted and his warm skin was beneath her palms.

He paused long enough to shrug out of the shirt and she reached for the hem of her blouse and started to work it up over her head. He finished removing the garment for her and then he joined their lips again in a long, searching kiss that took Clementine's breath.

Once he finally broke the contact of their lips, she sucked in needy breaths as she whispered, "Oh, Quito, I've never stopped wanting you. All these years—it's still the same."

He pulled back far enough to look at her and as

he did his fingers tenderly pushed a tumbled lock of blond hair off her brow. "It is for me, too, Clem. I've never wanted any woman like this. Like I do you."

The intensity on his face caused her breath to catch in her throat and for a split second the urge to weep nearly overcame her. Quito still wanted her. More than anyone else. She didn't deserve him. She didn't deserve to feel the glorious touch of his hands, his lips. Not after leaving him.

Thankfully she managed to stifle her sobs, but tears spilled from the corners of her eyes and leaked into her golden hair. Seeing them, Quito rubbed them away with his thumbs.

"My darling Clementine, why do you have tears?"

She breathed in deeply, then with a shake of her head she reached up and framed his jaws with her palms. "Because—I'm so sorry, Quito. I was so stupid. So foolish. Forgive me. Forgive me."

His dark features softened and he lowered his head to press his cheek against hers. "Shh. Don't. We're not going to talk about it anymore. That's in the past. This is now. And we're starting over."

*Starting over.* With every beat of her heart, the words chanted again and again inside her head. If only that were possible. If only she were once and truly free to start her life over. But she couldn't think about that now. She couldn't let that ominous shadow ruin these precious minutes she had with Quito.

"Yes," she murmured. "Let's put that behind us, Quito. All I want to do now is love you."

His lips covered hers and his hungry kiss told her he was in complete agreement and in only a matter of moments Clementine's mind was emptied of everything except the feel of his hands removing her bra, cupping her breasts and teasing her waiting nipples.

Like a thirsty sponge, she absorbed every kiss, every caress he was extolling on her body until she was filled with a desire so hot she could only moan and writhe beneath him.

"Are you trying to torture me?" she asked brokenly. "I'm on fire, Quito!"

Lifting his head, he looked at her through locks of crow-black hair. A grin that was almost savage exposed his white teeth and she was suddenly reminded of his Navajo/Mexican heritage. The heart of a warrior had been bred in his genes and if necessary he would fight fiercely to protect her. Just knowing that turned her heart to liquid love and she felt it pouring from her body and searching for a way to flow into him.

"Don't ask me to hurry, Clem. We're only starting."

She groaned, but it was a raw sound of pleasure and he dipped his head to her belly and lathed her skin with his tongue. At the same time he began to unbutton her low-rise jeans.

In spite of his warning to go slow, Clementine

lifted her hips so that he could ease the jeans down over her hips.

Quito smiled as he saw that she wasn't wearing any panties. "You're still a wicked woman I see."

A soft laugh gurgled in her throat. "Only you make me that way."

His eyes glinted as they connected with hers and then his hand slid down her belly to cup the intimate mound at the apex of her thighs.

She shivered with delight and ran her hands down his back. When her fingertips finally came to rest, she could feel the rigid flesh that had been torn and twisted by the bullets and was now mending into a jagged, dark blue scar.

Running her fingers along the deadly reminder, she looked into his face. He said nothing and neither did she. No words were needed to describe the fear and relief those scars represented.

"I love you, Clementine Jones."

She smiled at him and then she closed her eyes so that he couldn't see her tears.

"I love you, too," she whispered.

The words created a sudden, urgent fire between them and Quito left the bed long enough to shed his jeans and boots. When he returned to her, she spread her thighs and welcomed his body into hers.

Time ceased to exist as their bodies strained to satisfy, to give and take. Outside darkness settled over the high desert and inside on Quito's bed Clementine felt she was spiraling upward into the star-strung sky.

Sweat stung his eyes and his lungs burned for oxygen. Beneath him, he could feel the inner folds of her body clenching him tighter and tighter. Her legs, which were wrapped around his, were like bands of iron velvet holding him down and inside her. Pleasure, too sweet to describe, swirled around in his head and throughout his body.

He wanted these precious moments to go on forever and ever. But his body was a hungry traitor to his mind and soon he was spilling himself inside her, rocking their hips together with one final thrust.

The physical exertion drained him and he fell limply against her, his breathing rough and ragged.

"Quito! Oh, God! What have you done?"

Fear instantly washed away Clementine's lingering aftereffects of their lovemaking and she pushed at his shoulders until she rolled his back onto the mattress. Then kneeling over him, she wiped his damp forehead as he struggled to regain his breath.

His lips twisted into something between a grimace and a grin. "Do I have to tell you? I just made love to you and it's darned near killed me. That's what I've done."

With each word he spoke, his breathing became more normal and she let out a long sigh of relief. "I'm so sorry, Quito. I wanted it to be good for you."

Groaning, he lifted his hand to the back of her neck and pulled her down beside him. She snuggled her cheek against his bare shoulder as he murmured, "Believe me, Clem. It was plenty good. Too good."

Closing her eyes, she touched her fingers against his scarred ribs. "Does it still hurt here?" she asked.

His fingers began to play with her hair as his body began to relax. "No. It used to. But not anymore. I'm just short-winded. I guess I'm going to have to get back to jogging to get my lungs back in shape."

She opened her eyes and tilted her back just far enough to see his face. "Just don't do it on the road, okay?"

Puzzled by her request, he frowned at her. "Why not?"

Slipping her arm across his stomach, she hugged him. "Because. Some insane person tried to kill you on the highway. Just think what might have happened if you'd been out of your vehicle. You'd be a sitting target."

"Not exactly. I'd be a jogging target," he corrected.

She gave him a little shake. "Quito. That isn't funny. It's nothing to joke about. Please say you'll do your jogging here at the ranch or somewhere safe."

Rolling toward her, he put his arm around her shoulders and drew her up against the front of him. As he stroked her back with long, soothing motions, he said, "All right. I promise. I don't want you to worry about me. Ever."

"How could a woman not worry about a man who acts like Wyatt Earp?" she asked teasingly, but deep down she knew she would worry every waking hour about him. At least until the man who tried to kill him was caught and put behind bars for the rest of his life.

"Wyatt Earp lived to be a very old man," he said. "Probably because he had a good woman by his side."

Was Quito suggesting he wanted her to remain by his side? Clementine wondered. He'd told her he loved her. And in the heat of passion, she'd admitted that she loved him, too. Which was true. She'd never *stopped* loving him. But she wasn't so sure it had been a good thing to announce her feelings to him. He was going to expect her to stay here now. And that was one thing she just couldn't do. Not and keep the both of them safe.

"Have you made any headway in solving your shooting case?" she asked.

"No. But we did pick up a bit of a lead yesterday."

Their bodies were beginning to cool so Clementine pulled a sheet up to their waist. "Really? Why didn't you tell me before now?"

He brought his forehead against hers. "Because I haven't exactly had a chance. We've been busy on other subjects."

She chuckled softly. "No. I guess you haven't," she said. "So what was the lead? Anything promising?"

He drew in a long breath and released it. Clementine sensed the whole issue was weighing heavily on his mind and that bothered her. She wished more than anything that she could take all his worries away. That she could make him happy. Now and always.

"Just a death threat in the mail."

His words were such a shock to her that her head snapped back and she stared at his face in the growing darkness. "A death threat? Oh, God, Quito! What did it say? What are you going to do?"

Quito could feel her trembling and he almost wished he hadn't mentioned the note. But in the long run, he knew it wouldn't be good to try to sugarcoat the situation. Clementine needed to be aware of the seriousness of the threat. If nothing else, for her own safety.

"I don't remember the exact wording. But more or less that he was going to make sure the next time he'd get the job done."

Shivering, she lay her head down on his chest and pressed her ear against his heartbeat. "That terrifies me, Quito," she murmured. "If something happened to you—I couldn't bear it."

He circled his arms around her and breathed in the feminine scent of her moist skin. "It won't. We're going to get this guy. And when we do he'll not see the light of day again until he's so old he'll have to be led around by a nurse."

"Dear Lord, I hope you're right," she mumbled.

He trailed his fingertips over her soft nape. "The death threat could have been the shooter's mistake, Clementine. We might find DNA on the stamp or the envelope. They're examining it at the crime lab in Albuquerque now."

She tilted her head back to look at him and he could see a glimmer of hope in her eyes. At that moment he very much wanted to believe that she loved him. She'd said as much. But saying words were easy. Proving them was another thing.

"Do you think they'll find anything?"

He nodded. "I think so. But the real question will be whether the DNA will be listed in our crime bank."

"Well, why wouldn't it be?" she demanded. "He or, who knows, maybe some woman wants you dead. So he or she is a criminal," Clementine reasoned.

"True. But not all criminals are caught. Some are never caught in their lifetime. Or this person might have been a nice guy at one time and something made him suddenly twist off and buy a gun."

"Why use it on you, Quito? Have you made anyone that angry around here?"

He grimaced. "Not recently. But I've had a few swear to kill me in the past. It was all talk, though. Once they sobered up and got out of jail they remembered I was their friend." He bent his head and pressed his lips to the crown of her hair. "Let's not talk about it anymore," Quito whispered. "Are you getting hungry?"

"Are you?"

Her evasive answer caused him to chuckle. "I'm starving. But I don't want to get out of bed. Not when I have you here in my arms like this. It feels too good to move."

"Mmm. You're right," she said as she wiggled suggestively against him. "But if we don't get up and eat, we might wither away."

"I couldn't think of a better way to wither away," he murmured.

She smiled in the darkness and then her smile faded as she allowed her thoughts to turn toward tomorrow and the days following. How long could she risk staying here, she wondered. Could she chance a few weeks? And when they ended, how could she tell Quito that she had to leave?

Oh, God, she didn't want to think about it now. It was too painful and this was the first time in years that she'd felt any sort of happiness. She couldn't help but feel greedy enough to snatch all she could while she could.

Quickly, before he could stop her, she bounced to her feet and reached for her clothes. "Come on, lazy bones. You promised to cook me a steak. I want to see if you can cook as well you make love."

With a wicked little chuckle, he threw his legs over the side of the bed and bent down to retrieve his jeans. "Clementine, I promise you'll enjoy every bite."

Thirty minutes later the two of them were sitting on the back porch at a table made of bent willow branches with a glass top. The chairs were also made of bent willow, the seats cushioned with red pillows.

As promised, Quito had prepared steaks by searing them in a big iron skillet and letting them fry in their own juices. A New York strip for her and a T-bone for him. He'd prepared both pieces of meat rare, then added salad to their plates along with baked potatoes hurried in the microwave.

Clementine had never felt so ravenous. Normally eating was just a routine she forced herself to go through in order to remain healthy. But tonight she savored each bite as though she'd wakened from a coma and everything was brand-new, even the food on her plate.

Quito had lit three tall citronella lanterns near the table and the open flames flickered in the soft, westerly breeze. Across the way, she could hear the livestock tearing at the grass as they grazed along the fence separating the yard from the pasture.

"The quietness out here is so lovely, Quito. You must enjoy it after working all day."

"I do. But sometimes it can close in on me. There

have been times I've ended up talking to the cows and the horses. Guess they don't understand a thing I say, but the good part is they don't give me any sass," he joked.

She glanced down at her plate as she sliced a knife through the tender meat. "It's hard for me to imagine that you've gotten lonely. Your work keeps you so busy. And I know you have lots of friends. I'm sure they invite you out."

He nodded. "On occasion. But I'm not much of a goer. I like being home. I guess I'm boring."

If only Niles had been that way, she thought grimly. He'd wanted to socialize every single night of the week. He had definitely not been husband material. But then she hadn't realized that before their wedding had taken place. If she had, things might be entirely different now.

"Why are you frowning, Clem? You look like you've just bitten into a sour grape. I hope my cooking isn't that bad."

Wanting to reassure him, she reached over and squeezed his forearm that was resting on the table top. "It's not the food. The dinner is delicious. I was just thinking about, well, maybe I'd better not say."

"Go on," he urged. "I'd like to know what it is that can make you look so sad."

She glanced across the table at him and felt her breath catch in her throat. His strong, bronze features were bathed with flickering lantern light while the same glow left a sheen on the blue-black hair falling across his forehead. The passing years had matured his looks and honed him into the most masculine man she'd ever seen. Just looking at him set her temperature rising.

"I was just thinking how my ex-husband loved to party and socialize. I got so tired of dressing up, laughing and pretending to be happy. It was a strain, Quito. If I'd been a drinker, I would have turned into an alcoholic. As it was, I became a nervous wreck. I developed ulcers and insomnia."

His expression turned thoughtful. "He doesn't sound like the sort of man you would marry."

She made a disgusted sound in her throat. "I wouldn't have if I'd really known him. Before we got married he appeared to be the complete opposite. He talked about hearth and home and children. Most all the things that women long for. But he was just feeding me words that he knew I wanted to hear. Later, well, I don't want to talk about later. This night is too special." Her eyes softened with love as she picked up her glass and held it toward him. "Let's make a toast, Quito."

A faint smile touched his lips. "All right. What are we toasting?"

"Oh, I don't know." She smiled at him. "Just being happy, I guess."

"There's nothing wrong with that," he agreed.

She clinked her margarita against his then took a long sip of the icy drink. "To being happy. Now and always," she murmured.

And he would be happy, Quito thought, as long as Clementine was here with him, loving him, sharing her life with him. The questions that he needed to ask danced eagerly around his mind. Especially if she loved him enough to stay this time. But Quito couldn't bring himself to voice the question out loud. If her answer wasn't what he wanted to hear, the night would be ruined. His whole future would be ruined. He didn't want to risk spoiling this time with Clementine. For tonight, at least, he could pretend the two of them would live the rest of their lives together.

Both of them drained their glasses and as Quito set his back down on the tabletop, he glanced pointedly at her plate. "Are you finished eating?"

A suggestive smile dimpled her cheeks. "Why? Is it past your bedtime? If you're ready to take me home, I can forget about having coffee."

Reaching over, he curled his hand around hers. "Darling, you *are* home. I'm not taking you anywhere tonight. Except to bed."

Heat raced through her body. Anticipation sizzled along her skin and caused every muscle in her body to contract. How could she want him so, she wondered, when less than an hour ago he'd made thorough and complete love to her?

*Because he's the very essence of your being. Because you love him more than your own life.*

She couldn't argue with the little voice inside her. It had come from her heart. But acknowledging the depth of her feelings for Quito wouldn't fix things. Short of Niles disappearing from the face of the earth, she didn't know what could ever fix it.

Trying not to let herself dwell on that dour thought, she asked, "What about the coffee?"

Smiling slyly, he rose to his feet and gently pulled her from her chair. "We'll have that for breakfast."

## Chapter Eight

The next morning Quito cooked for her again. French toast with maple syrup and thick slices of slab bacon. The coffee was hot and delicious and by the time she'd finished her second cup and most of the food on her plate, she felt like she'd slept at least five hours instead of three.

"So, what are you going to do today?" Quito asked as they lingered at the table with their coffee cups. "You want me to drop you off at the Jones house?"

Nodding, she said, "Since my car is there, I'd better. I still have plenty of cleaning to do. And I think the power company will be out today to turn the electricity on."

Surprise arched his brows. "You're turning on all the utilities?"

"Why, yes. I can't stay there unless I have lights and water and all that." She made a helpless gesture with her hand. "Well, I suppose I could. These past two years I've learned how to rough it pretty well. But I don't see any need in doing that. I don't mind paying the connect fee. And as for the water, I'll have someone come out and make sure the pump on the well is still in working order."

His face was stoic. "I see. You're planning to stay there full-time. Rather than here."

Clementine tried not to flinch at the emptiness she heard in his voice. If only he knew how much she wanted to stay with him, full-time, she thought. If only she could tell him how she actually felt. But the moment she did, she would be committing herself. And she couldn't do that. Not when just being here might bring wrath down on both of them.

"Well, I suppose. You wouldn't want me getting underfoot here and I don't want to be a bother," she reasoned in a careful voice.

He placed his coffee cup on the table and leaned back in his chair to study her through narrowed eyes. At that moment Clementine understood what the term steely-eyed warrior meant. He might as well have painted stripes on his cheekbones because it was obvious he was about to go on the warpath.

"You see yourself as a guest here?" he asked far too quietly.

"Not exactly," she said, then shaking her head, she put her cup aside and leaned across the table toward him. "But, Quito, you have a job, a life apart from mine. I don't want to push myself into it."

"Who said you'd be pushing?"

"No one." She heaved out a heavy breath and started again. "Do you want me to stay here, with you?"

A muscle ticked in his jaw and then he shrugged. "Do whatever you want. You will anyway."

Clementine supposed she deserved that. She'd hurt him terribly. But how could she try to make it up to him now? To do that might eventually cause him far more hurt than happiness.

Tears were suddenly burning her throat as she stared wretchedly across the room. "You're sounding childish now," she finally managed to say.

"I think I have a right to."

She swallowed, then blinking at the moisture collecting in her eyes, she turned her gaze back to him. "Maybe it was a mistake for me to stay here last night," she said hoarsely. "Maybe you're expecting too much from me."

"I thought last night meant something to you."

Unable to face him any longer, Clementine rose

to her feet and walked over to a door leading outside. The top half was made of pane glass and she stared unseeingly at the rolling desert hills surrounding Quito's property.

"It meant everything to me," she said in a choked voice.

He didn't make any sort of reply and she was thinking he must be too angry to speak when his hands came down on the back of her shoulders. She hadn't heard him leave his chair or cross the room and his unexpected touch caused her to jump.

"I'm sorry, Clem." Bending his head, he nuzzled the side of her neck. "I know I'm acting possessively. And I know I don't have any right. But—" He paused as he slid his arms around her waist. "It's good to have you here with me. And I want us to have more time together. Is that so bad?"

A little cry sounded in her throat as she twisted in his arms and buried her face against his chest. His hard warm body instantly enveloped her with incredible pleasure and a sense of security that only he could give her.

"Oh, Quito. Please understand. I can't make any promises now. This is all so new. When I came up here I didn't plan on this happening with you and me. I need time to think about it." Lifting her face, she did her best to smile at him. "Besides, once I get the house all clean, I'd like for you to stay with me in the

Jones House. It's been empty too long. It needs some noise bounced off the walls."

Quito's arms tightened around her. "You mean you're not leaving soon?"

His question ripped at her heart and she had to swallow again before she could answer. "No. I don't want to leave anytime soon."

He released a heavy breath. "What about the trip you were planning to the Mexican mountains?"

"A definite date hasn't been set for the trip yet. And even when it is set, they don't necessarily need for me to be there in person. My funding is mostly what they need."

Easing back from her, he trailed his fingers down the side of her face. "I don't think I have to tell you what it means to me to have you back. All these years I knew that I would see you again. I just didn't know when or where."

Tilting her head back, she stared up at him in wonder. "How could you know that, Quito? So much time has passed. Eleven years. I wasn't even sure you would still be here."

A quizzical frown wrinkled his features. "This is my land, my home. The people of San Juan County depend on me to keep them safe. I would never leave this place."

Even for me, she thought. But she kept the words to herself. She didn't want them to start arguing again. She didn't want to ask him why he hadn't come to Houston all those years ago and demand that she return to New Mexico with him. For weeks and months after she'd moved back with her parents, she'd watched for him, prayed for him. She'd wanted him to come after her, to change her mind. But he was a man with great pride. And, after all, she'd told him not to follow her. She should have known he would respect her parting words.

"I'm very glad you were here," she whispered.

He bent his head and kissed her lips. "It's getting late. I'd better get to work. Or they'll think I've been bushwhacked."

She frowned as she stepped out of his embrace. "Quito! That isn't anything to joke about!" she scolded.

His face grim, he reached for his hat which was hanging on a peg by the door. "Who says I'm joking?"

After Quito dropped Clementine off at the Jones house, he hurried on to the sheriff's department and found his troop of deputies, along with his under sheriff, already gathered for the morning briefing.

"I thought we were going to have to send the cavalry out looking for you," Jess said under his breath as Quito took a seat beside him at the front of the room.

"Just running a little late," Quito muttered back.

From the corner of his eye, Jess cast him a sly glance. "I won't ask the reason for your tardiness."

"Thanks. I wouldn't have told you anyway," he said wryly, then his expression turned serious. "Has anything come back on the envelope?"

"I'm expecting to get the preliminary findings later this morning. I've ordered Redwing to keep calling until he gets an answer."

"Good," he said, then rising to his feet, he called the deputies to order and began the day's agenda.

Lunchtime was growing near when Jess knocked on the door of Quito's office.

He motioned for the under sheriff to enter.

"You have news?" he questioned before Jess had a chance to speak.

Jess nodded and sank onto the wooden chair sitting at an angle to Quito's desk. "Finally. They tell us the DNA belongs to a male."

"That's not much news. I hadn't expected a woman to be firing at me point-blank," Quito muttered.

Jess tried not to smile, but he did anyway. "I don't know about that. I'm pretty sure you've angered a few around town when you wouldn't go out with them."

"Hell," Quito cursed. "You make it sound like women come after me. I can't remember when that's ever happened."

Jess looked at the ceiling and whistled. "Oh, I'd say about three, four days ago."

Quito thought he was long past the age of blushing. But he could feel red heat crawling up his neck. "Clementine is different," he said gruffly.

"I'll say."

Quito shot him a steely glare.

Jess cleared his throat and crossed his ankles. "Uh, well, back to the test. So far forensics hasn't found a match in the data bank. But they plan to run it through again after the in-depth testing is completed."

"Hmmp," Quito grunted. "I don't expect they'll match it."

Jess looked at him curiously. "Why do you say that?"

Quito shrugged. "Not any certain reason. Just a hunch I have. Maybe it's just my Indian blood talking to me. I don't know. But I don't figure this man has a criminal record. He's probably been careful about getting caught. And I still have the feeling he was hired."

Jess grimaced. "Yeah. I kinda have that feeling, too. Sorta makes it even scarier somehow. To think two people plotted your death."

Quito let out a rough sigh. "There could be worse things."

Jess looked at him as though he'd just discovered his boss was crazy. Well, he was a little crazy, Quito thought. Thanks to Clementine for that malady. Even the fact that someone was trying to kill him came as a second thought to the Texas heiress.

Last night as they'd made love, he'd felt her giving body and heard her words of love. But this morning, he'd sensed a barrier between them. And when she'd talked about the Jones House he'd known that she wasn't expecting to stay around forever. If that had been her plans, she would have thrown her arms around him and promised to never, ever leave him. She hadn't done that. Instead she'd been evasive and he couldn't understand any of the mixed signals she'd been giving him.

He'd been a fool for ever making love to her again, he thought grimly. But he hadn't been able to help himself. And it was true that a wise man would never know the giddy pleasures of love. If he'd had any wisdom at all, he would have told her to tend to her business and get back to Houston where she belonged. But he loved her. *Loved her!* After eleven years, it was pretty obvious he wasn't going to be able to change that fact.

"I can't imagine what could be worse," Jess said, breaking into Quito's deep thoughts.

Quito leveled a stern gaze on his under sheriff. "Think about it, Jess. You'll come up with a lot worse things than someone trying to take your life."

His face puckered into a thoughtful frown, Jess was about to speak again, when the intercom on Quito's desk crackled.

"Sir, Neil Rankin is here. Can you see him now?" his secretary asked.

There were a million things he needed to be

doing. One in particular was meeting with the city's mayor about an upcoming festival. A parade had been scheduled and Quito was going to have to deal with a lot of extra security problems. There was also a case his detectives were presently working on that involved a series of serious robberies. He believed the crimes had crossed over into Texas and, if so, he was going to have to call in the FBI, or at the very least the Texas Rangers. And that was something he didn't want to have to do. His men worked diligently for him. He didn't want them to get the idea that they were somehow failing to get the job done.

"Yeah. Send him in," he told her, then turned his attention back to Jess. "Thanks for the report, Jess. I guess it's just a waiting game now. Is anyone still working on the tag number?"

Rising from his chair, Jess said, "I gave that job to Olin. Since he only has two numbers to work with, it's going slowly."

Quito nodded. "Okay. What about the south county robberies? Is Redwing getting anywhere with that?"

Jess nodded. "He's headed down to Dalhart this afternoon. He thinks some of the horses might have ended up there."

"Good. Tell him to take another man if he needs him," Quito said.

As Jess nodded, Neil knocked on the door and sauntered in before Quito could answer.

After greeting the lawyer, Jess said, "You two go ahead. I've got work to do."

"So do I," Quito muttered for Neil's benefit. "But this guy doesn't seem to realize it. What are you doing here? This is twice you've visited my office in the past few days. Do I look like I'm sick and need to be checked on or something?"

Neil chuckled and taking hold of the chair Jess had been using, he turned the straight-back toward Quito's desk, then straddled the seat. "Well, actually you do look a bit peaked this morning. What's wrong? No sleep?"

Quito refused to look at him. "I don't have time to discuss my sleeping habits with you this morning, old friend."

"Boy, you sound out of sorts this morning. What's wrong?"

Everything was wrong, Quito thought. He was repeating the same old mistake he'd made with Clementine eleven years ago. He was going to have to go through that same ripping pain of losing her again. He could feel the devastation coming and he didn't know any way to stop it.

"What you need is some lunch at the Wagon Wheel. Come on," he invited as he jumped to his feet. "I'm buying."

After the heavy breakfast Quito had shared with Clementine, he wasn't feeling any sort of hunger pains. But Neil was one of his best friends and he didn't want to offend him.

"All right. I guess I could eat a burger or something."

Quito grabbed his hat and the two men quickly left the building. As they walked down the sidewalk toward the old diner, Quito asked, "Neil, when Clem talked to you about the Jones House, did she say she was going to sell it, or what?"

Neil shrugged a shoulder. "Said she hadn't made up her mind. But the day we discussed the place was the first day she'd gotten back here," he reasoned. "I imagine she's been thinking things through since then. And I have a feeling that Ms. Jones will be sticking around for good this time."

Quito grimaced. "I doubt it."

Neil jerked his head toward his friend. "Why do you say that? I'll bet she hasn't said that to you."

"Not in so many words. But I can feel it. Hell," he added crossly. "I don't want to talk about Clem. I don't know why I brought her up anyway."

"Hmm. Sorry, old man. Have you seen her lately?"

Quito nearly sputtered at his question. "Uh, yes. And no, we didn't have an argument or anything like that. Forget it," he said with a shake of his head. "Let's go eat."

By now the two men had reached the front of the Wagon Wheel. Before Neil reached to open the plate-glass door, he patted Quito's shoulder. "Women are not to be taken seriously, Quito. You follow my motto and you'll not be going around feeling like you've been dropped into hell."

Quito growled at him. "You have a horrible track record with women. Why should I take advice from you?"

Neil laughed. "Because I'm your best buddy in the world."

The power utility truck was lumbering back down the mountain as Clementine walked into the house. The first thing she was going to do now that she had electricity was to turn on the air conditioner. Thankfully, each year, her father had hired a maintenance man to make sure the plumbing and the heating and cooling system of the house were in working order.

She was setting the thermostat when her cell phone rang.

Since Quito, Oscar and her parents were the only people who had the number, she figured it had to be Oscar. She couldn't see her parents calling from Italy or Greece, or whichever place they were hopscotching to.

"Hello?"

"Clem, it's Oscar. Hope I'm not disturbing you."

She sat down on the end of the couch, a red floral chintz that would hopefully look beautiful again once she ran a vacuum cleaner over it.

"Not at all. What's up?"

He didn't respond immediately and Clementine could feel a cloud of dread creeping over her as she waited for him to answer.

"Oscar? Has Niles shown up at your office again?"

"No. No. It's not that. Sorry I'm hesitating. I was just trying to find the right words to tell you about this. But I guess there's not any right words."

She gripped the phone. "Okay. Just tell me."

"Don't get alarmed, Clementine, but someone broke into your house last night."

"What?" She didn't realize she'd whispered the word until Oscar asked her to repeat what she'd just spoken.

"Oscar, did you say someone broke into my house?"

"Sorry, Clem. But that's it. The police called me after a neighbor reported seeing the lights on. Apparently your neighbor must have known you were gone."

Her mind was suddenly whirling with questions. "That must have been Geneva. She keeps a watch on things for me when I'm out of town. But why did she have to call the police?" Clementine demanded. "Why didn't the alarm system go off?"

"Someone disabled it."

Clementine cursed under her breath. "Damn it, Oscar, I spent a fortune on that security system. If it isn't going to work—" She suddenly stopped as more questions invaded her mind. "Okay, lay it on me. What was stolen? The television? Everything electronic? Or did they manage to break into the safe where I store my jewelry?"

"No. And no. So far as I can tell, nothing was taken."

Clementine was so surprised, she unconsciously rose to her feet and began pacing around the room.

"Okay, Oscar, just back up and begin again. Someone broke into my house, but nothing appears to be taken? That's crazy! Did the alarm eventually go off and scare them away?"

"No. As I told you before, the alarm was totally disabled. Whoever did it, wasn't dumb."

She shivered at the very thought of someone in her house, going through her private things. "What do the police think?"

Oscar sighed. "They dusted for prints, but they don't expect to find any. Some of your things—your intimate wear was scattered around the bedroom. And some of your costume jewelry was spilled onto the dresser. The police suspect it might be the acts of a group of randy teenage boys. But I told them I had other ideas."

Frowning, Clementine paused in her pacing.

"I think Niles is the culprit," Oscar continued. "That's what worries me about the whole thing."

Clementine suddenly felt ice cold even though the air conditioner hadn't had nearly enough time to cool the huge house.

"Oh, God, Oscar. Please, please don't tell me— that bastard was in my house, going through my things. I can't stand it!"

"I'm sorry, Clem. You asked."

Wiping a shaky hand across her face, she said, "Tell me, Oscar, exactly what in my house was disturbed?"

"It would be hard to say, Clem. Whoever did the deed could have put some things back. Like I said, your underclothes were strewn everywhere. As though the person was obsessed with your body or fantasized about making love to you. God, this is embarrassing just even talking about it," he muttered. "You're just like my own daughter. And I'd like to choke whoever did this."

"Don't worry about embarrassing me, Oscar. We're old friends. You know that you can say anything to me."

"Well, actually, that's about all there is to tell."

"Do I need to fly down there? Do the police need to see me?"

"No. No," he quickly assured her. "Coming back to Houston is the last thing you need to do. I've assured the police that I'm your lawyer and director of your family affairs. They can get any information they need from me."

Clementine felt ill. Although, she didn't know why. Every day people had their homes broken into, their personal things destroyed or stolen. This incident with her house was no worse. And for God's sake, it wouldn't have been Niles, she mentally argued. There wasn't any point in him breaking in when he knew she wasn't at home.

"Clem?"

"Hmm?"

"You're not speaking. What are you thinking?" Oscar asked worriedly.

"Nothing. I mean, I was just thinking it couldn't be Niles, Oscar. He has no reason to break in. I'm not there for him to harass, to curse at, or slap around."

"Yes, but he doesn't know where you are. He probably thought he could find something, some clue inside your house that would lead him to you."

"I'm always careful not to leave a trail of information behind me." Her legs were beginning to feel so spongy that she was forced to return to her seat on the couch. "Uh, Oscar, are you sure the safe wasn't opened?"

"It was locked. I opened it to make sure none of your jewels were missing. Nothing looked amiss."

She released a ragged breath. "I'd placed a silk-covered box in there. Did you see it?"

"Yes. But I didn't open it. Why?"

She swallowed as she thought of the three items she'd cherished for all these years. A love letter from Quito. A small lock of his black hair. And the first badge he'd ever worn as sheriff. Even after she'd married Niles, she had not been able to toss those things away. It would have been like throwing a part of herself away. So she'd hid them within some other family items, knowing that Niles would never go through them. Family history had been one of the least important matters to him. But now, if Niles had found the letter with Quito's name on it... She shuddered as her thoughts trailed away and refused to picture the worst.

"I had some sentimental pieces inside that box. Things that I would never want Niles to see."

"I don't think the safe was bothered. But I can't be sure. The police did dust it for prints, but they're not expecting to find any. Gloves easily take care of those. I just think you ought to start watching over your shoulder," Oscar warned.

Niles had already tried beating her to make her come back to him. She supposed in his sick mind the next step would be killing her to prevent another man from having her, something he'd often threatened to do. But there could be worse things than that, she thought. He could turn his sadistic evilness on Quito. And if that should ever happen, she'd never be able to forgive herself.

## Chapter Nine

Later that day, long after Oscar's ominous call, Clementine gathered herself together and drove into Aztec. She needed linens for the bed and the bathrooms, groceries to stock the kitchen, plus cooking utensils. Thankfully her mother had left behind a perfectly good set of dishes and silverware, so she needn't bother with those.

Making the house fit to live in again was something she'd been looking forward to. And though she wasn't a big shopper, she'd been excited about picking out towels and sheets, spatulas and mixing bowls. But some of her pleasure had been dampened by

Oscar's call and she chewed on the information he'd given her all the way into town.

So far it wasn't a fact that Niles had been the person in her house. That was only Oscar's supposition. But she had a sinking feeling that the lawyer was right. Ninety-nine percent of the time Oscar was right about things. That's why her father had hired him many, many years ago. He'd respected the man's instincts.

What would it mean if Niles had broken into her home, she asked herself. If he hadn't found the box with her keepsakes from Quito, she couldn't think of anything else that would lead him here. She'd carefully erased every message on her answering machine. She had not left any paper notes by the phone or on the fridge. She'd given notice to the post office to hold all her mail. There was no way Niles could follow her trail.

By the time Clementine had pulled into the parking lot of a discount store, she felt a bit perkier and as she walked toward the entrance, she forced herself to look up at the wide blue sky and smile. She was here, after all. Here with Quito. That was enough to make her happy.

It took her over two hours to finish her shopping and since it was so late, she decided to stop by the sheriff's office to see if Quito was nearly finished for the day. If he hadn't gotten the message this morning that she wanted him to stay with her in the Jones House, she intended to repeat it.

Which was probably a mistake, she thought sadly. Continuing a physical relationship with Quito would only make things worse once she had to say good-bye. She realized he construed their being together as being together for always. And under any other circumstance he would be right. More than anything she wanted to spend the rest of her life with Quito. But she couldn't make him such a promise now. And she didn't know how she was going to make him understand without telling him about Niles.

A young male officer named Justin was on duty at the front desk and he eyed Clementine with appreciation as she inquired about the sheriff.

"Sorry, ma'am. Sheriff Perez is out on a call. I don't look for him to be back anytime soon. There's been a shooting over toward Shiprock and he went to help with the investigation."

Clementine frowned. "Oh. Isn't Shiprock on the reservation? I'd think the tribal police would be handling that. From what I understand they usually resent outside law."

"Usually that's the case. But Sheriff Perez is half Navajo. They consider him one of their own and he's good friends with the tribal policemen. They value his help."

"I see," she said as her spirits sank once again. Obviously she wouldn't be seeing Quito tonight. "Thank you anyway."

"Would you like to leave him a message?" the officer offered as though he could read disappointment in her face.

She smiled wanly. "Just tell him Clementine dropped by."

Except for one dim light, the big house on the hill was dark. But in spite of the very late hour, Quito was certain Clementine was home. Her car was parked near the rock steps.

He climbed them slowly, tiredly, until he crossed the short yard and walked up on the porch. Calling her name, he rapped his knuckles against the closed door.

Only seconds later, he heard the rapid thud of her feet as she hurried to the door. And after a quick peek through the small window on the door, she pulled back the wooden panel and smiled at him as though he was the most special thing on earth.

Hungrily his eyes drank in the sexy sight of her blond hair piled upon her head and spilling from a messy bun. The shiny strands fell onto the white cotton robe covering her tall, curvy body. The ruffled neckline veed low between her breasts and exposed just enough skin to make his fingers beg to reveal more. But it was the warm light in her blue eyes that heated him the most.

"Quito! I had given up on seeing you tonight!" she

exclaimed with surprise. Stepping back, she motioned him in. "I was told you'd gone to Shiprock."

"I did go. I just made it back," he said as he moved past her. She smelled like lilac blossoms and some underlying musky scent that shouted she was a woman. Quito simply wanted to turn and pull her into his arms. But that would tell her just how eager he was to have her again and he didn't want her to know just how smitten, how consumed with her he'd always been. If she had to leave with his heart again, at least he could hang on to his pride.

"Justin told me you'd dropped by the office."

Clementine shut the door behind her and on second thought, locked it. Niles might not know where she was, but there was still someone out there who'd tried to kill Quito. As far as she was concerned it would be negligent not to be careful.

"I did. I went to town today to do some shopping for the house. And I stopped by to see if you were nearly finished with work. Obviously you weren't."

He nodded and she could see the lines of weariness around his eyes and mouth. At that moment it struck her just how very much she wanted to soothe him, love him, to make everything about his life better. Yet she feared that the more she touched, the more she loved, the more she would eventually hurt him.

"Yeah," he said. "It's a long drive from Shiprock to here in the dark. You have to keep a keen eye out for antelope and deer on the highway. One of the law officers there tried to get me to stay the night. But I told him I wanted to make it back home."

And back to her? she wondered. No. She couldn't let herself start thinking she was the axis of Quito's world. It would only start making her dream and want all the things she couldn't have.

Slipping her arm through his, she led him into the living room and toward the chintz couch where a lamp glowed at one end. "Come and sit down," she told him. "You must be exhausted."

He sank onto the middle cushion and Clementine stood in front of him and motioned for him to give her his foot.

"Let me pull off your boots," she said.

One black eyebrow arched upward beneath the brim of his gray Stetson. "You mean I'm staying here tonight?"

Laughing softly, she said, "I wouldn't want you to stay anywhere else."

As she dealt with his boots, he pulled off his hat and tossed it on the end table nearest to him.

"I am tired," he conceded as she placed his boots at the end of the couch.

"What about hungry?" she asked. "Have you eaten?"

She was treating him like a husband, Quito thought. And he didn't understand it. This morning she'd told him she needed to go slowly, to think about things. Yet she clearly wanted him with her. Were her mixed signals just those of a fickle woman or was there some underlying reason for her vacillating attitude? he wondered. Whatever the cause, it was driving him crazy.

"No. I haven't had time. But don't bother making me anything," he added quickly. "It's too late to be messing up the kitchen."

She laughed again. "Who cares if the kitchen is messed up? Remember, my mother doesn't live here anymore. I can stack dirty dishes to the ceiling if I want to. And I just might want to," she added with a dimpled grin.

A wan smile quirked his lips. "Hmm. You're feeling sassy tonight. You must have had a nice day."

"I'm sure it was better than yours," she said. "You can tell me all about it after I fix you something to eat."

She left the room and Quito leaned his head back against the couch and closed his eyes. The day had been long. It seemed like hours and hours had passed since he'd eaten lunch with Neil at the Wagon Wheel. He'd barely finished the meal with his friend when his pager had gone off and he'd discovered that Yuma Spottedhorse needed him over on the reservation.

Normally he wouldn't have involved himself in one of Yuma's investigations, but his friend had asked

for his help and he wasn't about to turn his back on
a fellow Navajo.

Quito was close to dozing off when Clementine's
quiet tread returned to the living room. Lifting his
eyelids, he was surprised to see that she was carrying a meal on a tray.

"Clem, I'm not that tired. I can eat at the table,"
he protested.

"Nonsense," she said with a gentle smile. "You
can sit right here and eat. Just be careful with the iced
tea. I filled the glass too full."

She carefully placed the tray on his lap and then so
she wouldn't shake the couch, she sat down at his feet.

The plate she'd served him was filled with warm
tamales topped with shredded longhorn cheese. Next
to those were two tacos, soft, flour tortillas oozing
with meat and sour cream.

He first attacked the tamales. "Did you already
have this prepared?" he asked as he shoveled a fork-
ful toward his mouth.

"I cooked it for myself. Leftovers, so don't worry,"
she teased. "I didn't knock myself out over the
stove."

He smiled and she scooted closer so that her
shoulder was resting against the side of his leg. His
first inclination was to reach over and stroke her
shiny hair, but he didn't. He knew that once he
touched her there would be no more food or words.

The idea surged excitement through him and pushed away all the weariness he'd been feeling on his drive back from Shiprock.

"What did you buy today?" he asked as he continued to eat.

"Sheets, towels, food, all the things I needed to stay here comfortably," she told him. "The house has cooled down now that the air conditioner has been turned on. Feels nice, huh?"

"Very nice."

"Your officer told me there had been a shooting over on the Navajo reservation. Was anyone hurt or killed?"

"Killed, unfortunately. A thirty-three-year-old male."

"That's terrible. What happened? Do you know yet?"

Quito shook his head. "Not yet. But it looks like there was drinking involved and a woman. The shooter is still on the loose and Yuma thinks he's headed up into Mesa Verde to try to lose himself in the mountains there. Or he might have stopped on the Ute reservation and talked a friend or someone he knows into hiding him there."

"You know who this man is?" he asked.

Quito shook his head. "Yuma has a suspect in mind. But neither one of us can be sure."

"Mesa Verde is a National Park," Clementine said,

twisting her head around and looking up at him with concern. "If a killer is running lose there—well, it would be awful."

"It would be worse than awful if a tourist was taken hostage by a dangerous criminal. But we're not sure if that's where he's gone or not. In the meantime, Yuma is out with his tracking dogs."

Clementine suggested thoughtfully, "Maybe this Yuma ought to call in the FBI for help."

Quito laughed. "Not Yuma Spottedhorse. It chafed him enough just to ask for my help. He'd rather eat fried crow than step aside to the white man's government agency." He took a long drink of the iced tea, then looked down at her. "But that's enough about the shooting. Tell me what else you did today."

She shifted around so that she was facing him and looped her arm around his jean-covered leg. Touching him had become a delicious habit. One that she had no inclination to break. Having him close steadied her in ways that nothing or no one ever had. Feeling the warmth of his body next to hers made her believe that everything was going to turn out right and good.

"Oh, nothing special. You'd think it was all boring stuff."

"As long as you enjoyed it, that's all that matters."

Her eyes fell to the cushion next to him as a dismal expression crossed her face. "I did enjoy it. But, well, I wasn't going to tell you about this, Quito. You already have enough of this sort of thing to deal with. But I guess I'll tell you anyway. Maybe it will help me get it off my mind."

His expression grew serious as he studied her drawn features. "What? What's wrong? You look upset."

She nodded solemnly. "I have been," she admitted. "Earlier this morning, I received a call from Oscar. He's a lawyer in Houston and a friend of the family. He works for my father in a legal and business way. Sees that everything is running smoothly, that sort of thing. And he sort of acts as a stand-in father for me."

Quito nodded that he understood. "Okay. What was this call about? Your parents?"

Clementine shook her head, then pushed at the fallen hair that had dipped over her eye. "No. They're fine. Um, someone broke into my house last night. The police were called out and Oscar was contacted."

His face suddenly grim, Quito raised up from his relaxed position against the couch. "What was taken?"

"Nothing," Clementine said bleakly. "As far as Oscar can tell nothing was taken. Only my…my undergarments were strewn everywhere. And I suppose some of them might have been taken."

A deep frown furrowed Quito's brow. "Sounds

like the perp was a pervert. Have you noticed any-one following you, calling you? That sort of thing?"

Only Niles, she thought bitterly. But that had been going on for years now. "No. Besides, Quito, I've been gone. I'd only been home from Afghanistan for less than a week when I left to drive up here."

He was silent for several thoughtful moments be-fore he finally said, "That worries me, Clem. Do you need to go check on things? If you do, I can go with you. Jess will be glad to take care of the office while I'm away."

Dear God, how wonderful it would be to always have strong, capable Quito to take care of her. Since she'd been a very young child, it seemed as though she'd been on her own. Of course, she had parents who'd always been good to her. But there had been many more times than not that she'd needed them and they had been away on pleasure trips, business trips, or at work and social events. She'd gotten used to taking care of herself and whatever needs or wor-ries she'd been presented with. So Quito's offer to help was very precious to her.

Clementine slowly shook her head. "Oscar says there isn't any need for me to drive back down there. He's taking care of everything. At least, what little can be done." She drew in a long breath and let it out. "And I suppose nothing was harmed. I need to for-get it."

"Look, Clem, anytime someone's house is invaded it *is* something. And frankly, I'm glad that you weren't there to find it that way. You would have felt very violated to see your things had been gone through by some stranger. Especially your intimate clothing. The bastard. He needs to be—well, I won't say what he needs in my opinion. At the very least he needs to be caught."

She studied his angry face. "You don't think it was teenagers?"

Shaking his head, he stabbed his fork into one of the tamales on his plate. "No. Teenagers always take things. Especially things they can sell. This person who broke into your house has—" Breaking off he lifted his head and leveled his dark eyes on her. "He has you on his mind."

Oh, God, help her, he was saying all the things Oscar had been saying. Only Quito didn't know that Niles was obsessed with her, that he'd vowed to get her back one way or the other.

A violent shiver rolled down her back and she tightened her arm around his leg. "Quito, I don't want to talk about it anymore. Okay? I'm here with you and that's more than a thousand miles away. It doesn't matter."

His dark eyes were gentle as he reached out and stroked the top of her head. "All right, honey. We'll put it aside for now."

She encouraged him to finish his meal and once he was finished, she carried the tray into the kitchen and made a fresh pot of coffee.

When it had finished dripping, she carried two cups back out to where Quito was still resting on the couch.

"If you feel up to it," she said, "let's take our coffee out on the back patio and I'll show you some of what I've been doing today."

Grinning lazily at her, he reached for his boots. "After a long day's work, I always like to take midnight strolls."

She pulled a face at him. "If I didn't think you were teasing, I'd throw this coffee right on you," she warned good-naturedly.

Chuckling, Quito rose to his feet and reached to take one of the cups from her hand. "I am. Don't get your hackles up."

Smiling, she took him by the hand and led him through a sliding glass door and onto a red stone patio. A halogen light with a sensor blinked on the moment they stepped past the door and flooded the whole backyard with a soft, yellow glow.

"See, I've been doing all sorts of cleaning," she said, waving her arm around her. "This whole place was piled with dead leaves and limbs. I raked them all up and carried them away. And then I started on the pool. That took even longer."

"You've been cleaning the pool?" he asked with surprise.

She urged him toward the kidney-shaped swimming pool that ran for at least thirty feet along the back of the house. A garden hose was thrown over the side and Quito could hear water trickling.

"I've not only cleaned it, I've been filling it. I bought chemicals today. So as soon as it gets full, we can jump in." She laughed then. "But you and I both know it will take a day or two for it to fill."

He sipped his coffee and tried to ignore the lifting of his spirits. If she was filling the pool that meant she was going to stay for a while, at least. The idea ought not make him so happy. If he had any gumption at all, he'd simply tell her he didn't have time for fun and games and just walk away. But his heart was in her hands and her body was like a sinful drug to him. He couldn't get enough of her. He'd never be able to get enough of her.

"My, my," he murmured. "You have been busy. I honestly didn't know you had this work ethic in you."

Playfully wrinkling her nose, she pretended to push him toward the pool. Instead she squeezed his hand and urged him over to a lawn swing with a padded seat.

They sank onto the swing together and Quito pushed it into a gentle motion as they sipped from their coffee cups. The night was unusually warm for the high desert, a slight breeze drifting in from the west. The Jones property extended three miles in all directions. Not a huge lot for western standards, especially for Texas folks, but it was a nice plot of land, which with a lot of work could be turned into a small ranch.

There had been many a time that Clementine had dreamed of doing just that. Of turning this place into a horse ranch and hopefully winning Quito back to her side.

Well, he was at her side again. What was she going to do now? she challenged herself with the question. What could she do?

The motion of the swing stopped abruptly and she looked over to see Quito bending down to place his empty cup to one side.

"Here," she told him. "You can put mine down, too. Or I'll be awake all night."

He looked at her, his mouth slanted in a sexy grin. "Maybe that's the way I want you to be," he murmured.

Heat colored her face as if she were a fifteen-year-old. "Quito, I—"

Reaching over, his fingertips traced the smooth skin exposed along the ruffle of her robe. Shivers of delight raced over her, causing goose bumps to rise all over her body.

"Clem, this morning I was being—" He stopped, shook his head, then started again. "I was being possessive and unreasonable. I hope you're not upset with me."

With a tiny groan, she leaned into him. "Oh, Quito, I wasn't upset. I could never be angry with you. I just want you to understand and I don't know how to make you see that things aren't exactly simple for me."

He pulled her head against his shoulder and stroked the back of her head. "It doesn't matter right now. That's what I'm trying to tell you. If you need time, if you have to go back to Houston, it's all right. I've waited for eleven years. I can wait longer if I have to."

Her heart was suddenly so full of love she was certain it was going to burst. "I want to do things right this time, Quito. Just give me a chance to do that."

His fingers continued to stroke tenderly over her hair and she began to relax and respond to his touch rather than the worries winding round and round in her mind.

"Clementine, I understand that you've been away from here for a long time. You've been married to another man and had a life far away from mine. I don't expect you to still be madly in love with me after all that. Hell, I wished it could be that way. But it's enough right now just to have you here in my arms."

Clementine couldn't stand it another second. She couldn't bear for him to keep thinking all the wrong things about her.

Lifting her head from his shoulder, she looked into his face and suddenly tears of emotion stung her eyes and forced her to swallow. "But I do love you madly, Quito. I always have. Always."

## Chapter Ten

Quito stared at her, his expression incredulous, his hands gripping her shoulders.

"What—Clem, you don't expect me to believe that, do you? Damn it, you've been gone for eleven years! If you loved me so much where were you? Why didn't you let me in on it?"

He sounded flabbergasted and a little angry and Clementine supposed she couldn't blame him.

Framing his face with both hands, she shook her head and searched his face with pleading eyes. "Forgive me, Quito. As I told you before, I've made such a mess of things! When I left here I thought I could get over you. I thought I could somehow stop my heart from grieving for you. I married Niles thinking it was the right thing to do, that I belonged in his and my parents' rich world and that eventually I would forget you. I had plans to keep busy with social functions and raise children and forget that I ever knew a Quito Perez. It didn't turn out that way. I guess Niles could always tell there was something standing between us. And that something was you."

Regret, real and painful, crumpled his face. "Oh, Clem. I'm so sorry. Sorry for you, for both of us."

Her tears found their way onto her cheeks and she wiped at them with the back of her fingers. "I don't expect you to be able to forgive and forget overnight," she whispered. "But just give us a chance, Quito. No matter what I say or do in the coming days, just remember that I love you. Will you do that?"

A puzzled frown crossed his face. "Clem, you sound like you're expecting something to happen. Why? What are you keeping from me?"

Terrified that he might guess what was going on in her head, she pulled out of his arms and left the lawn swing. Walking to the edge of the pool, she stared down at the dark water and struggled to gather her resolve. She had to be strong. If she admitted her fear of Niles to him, she knew without a doubt that Quito would go on a manhunt. He would hunt him down and then what might happen was too horrific for her to imagine.

"Clem? I asked you a question?"

His husky voice was right behind her and before he could get a good look at her teary face, she slid her arms around his waist and pressed her cheek to his chest. "Quito, I'm just being silly. I guess I'm just so happy that we're back together that I'm afraid something will happen to tear us apart. Please don't let that happen, Quito. Please!"

Sliding his arms around her, he buried his face against her warm neck. "Darling, darling," he murmured gently. "Nothing is going to happen. There's no sense in all this fretting you're doing."

He felt so warm and solid, so loving and gentle that she quickly began to relax in his arms. And after a few moments she lifted her head and studied his rugged face. "What are we doing wasting time out here when I'm dying to show you my new sheets."

A chuckle rumbled deep in his chest and he playfully swatted her bottom. "As long as you're lying naked on them, they'll be beautiful," he murmured slyly.

Laughing softly, she took him by the hand and led him into the house.

The upstairs bedroom she took him to was the one she'd used all those years ago when she and her parents had lived in the house. She'd mopped and dusted every nook and cranny, polished the furniture and, along with the new sheets, added a fluffy white comforter to the bed.

At the head of the bed, she clicked on a small lamp, then went to pull the shades at the windows.

Quito began unbuttoning his shirt as he watched her. "What is that for?" he asked with faint amusement. "We're out here in the wilds, away from everyone."

Clementine didn't look at him as she continued to make sure the blinds were shut. "You never know. Someone was out to get you at one time—we don't know if he'll try again."

"Gee, that's just what a man likes to hear before he makes love. That it might be his last time because tomorrow some sadistic maniac might kill him. Damn, Clem, when did you get so morbid? I don't remember you being so wary and worried."

When I had to start fighting for my own life, she thought grimly.

He let his khaki shirt fall to the floor and her gaze took in his bronze, muscled chest, the apparent strength of bare arms. He was the most beautiful, masculine man she'd ever known and as she went to him, she didn't allow her eyes to linger on the jagged scar running along his ribs. She wanted to put all that out of her mind and pretend that for tonight, at least, that nothing was wrong, that the rest of their lives were going to be just as this moment.

"Forget about that," she whispered as she went up

on her tiptoes and angled her mouth toward his. "And kiss me."

Her provocative order didn't have to be repeated and soon the mating of their lips became a bold, hungry union that set both of them on fire. And as he began to undress her, as his hands began to worship the satiny curves of her body, Clementine realized her life would be over if she didn't have this man in it.

The next morning Clementine woke to realize dawn had come and gone and the space beside her in the bed was empty.

Stiff and exhausted, she pushed herself out of bed and hurried out to the kitchen in hopes that she would find Quito there making breakfast, or at the least, brewing a pot of coffee.

Instead she found a half-empty pot that was so old it smelled like burned rubber. She poured out the foul smelling contents and turned to the cabinet for a filter. It was then the corner of her eye caught the note attached to the refrigerator door.

Dropping the coffeemaker's basket, she hurried across the small space and snatched the paper from the appliance.

It read:

Clementine, Sorry I had to leave so early. I'd planned to cook breakfast for you. But Yuma needs my help with a hostage situation. See you when I get back, Quito.

Clementine sank onto a kitchen bar stool as she felt the air drain out of her. Quito had gone to help with a hostage situation. This was not how she'd expected the morning to start. After the night they'd shared, she'd wanted to talk with him over breakfast, to make sure he still understood that her feelings weren't fleeting. Instead he'd gone off to some dangerous job where bullets could be flying.

Sighing, she slid off the stool and quickly began to gather the rest of the makings for the coffee.

While the brew dripped, she paced worriedly around the room. She couldn't continue on like this, she told herself. Eventually Quito was going to pressure her for answers and how could she tell him that the way wasn't clear for them to be married? That her ex-husband would be standing in the way with a knife or gun, or any weapon he could get his hands on to prevent her from having any happiness with another man.

Even if she did tell Quito about Niles, she didn't think he would understand the gravity of the situation. He would probably think a few threats from the law or a restraining order would take care of things. But those tactics had been used on Niles long before and they had not had the power to stop him from finding her, threatening her, and harassing her until she was forced to run and run and hide.

He'd been thrown in jail twice for ignoring a restraining order she'd had against him. The short amount of time Niles had been forced to spend behind bars hadn't done anything but made him angrier with her. He was a highly successful businessman in Houston. He was well-known in all the social circles and everyone believed he was a stand-up guy. No doubt he'd been forced to hand out plenty of payoffs to make sure his short stints in a jail cell hadn't leaked to the media and that his reputation would remain stellar.

No, as far as Clementine was concerned, restraining orders were useless as a weapon against Niles. She had to think of some other way to stop his stalking and the only way she could imagine doing that was to kill him. But she couldn't murder another human being. No matter how much she hated the man.

Eventually she realized the coffee was finished brewing and she poured herself a cup and dropped a piece of bread into the toaster.

She was sitting at the bar, slowly munching the small breakfast and wondering how she could get something on Niles, some sort of incriminating information she could use as leverage against him when her cell phone rang.

Since she'd given Quito the number a few days

ago, she desperately hoped to hear his voice on the other end as she snatched up the instrument and pushed a button to receive the call.

"Hello."

"Well, well, I finally get to hear my wife's lovely voice."

The sound of Niles' sick drawl shocked her so badly that she dropped the phone onto the tiled floor. The instrument clattered and bounced for several feet before it finally came to a rest beneath the edge of the cabinet.

She hurried over to the cell phone and as she bent down to pick it up, she could hear Niles shouting on the other end.

"Damn you, Clementine! Pick up the phone, you bitch, or you'll regret it later!"

Clenching her jaw with resolve, Clementine picked up the phone and with a shaky hand placed it against her ear. "Sorry, Niles," she pretended to apologize. "I accidently dropped the phone."

"Hmmp. Surprised to hear from me, no doubt."

She had to play this cool and calm, she told herself. If she acted just a smidgen congenial, he might start talking and she could perhaps get him to reveal how much he knew of where she'd been and where she was now.

"Well, actually, I am," she replied. "How did you get this number?"

His low laugh was a sadistic sound that made her skin crawl and she couldn't believe this was the same man who'd courted her in a gentlemanly fashion. When the two of them had married, she'd truly believed he'd cared about her. And maybe he had at one time. But over the course of their marriage he'd changed drastically into a demonic stranger.

"Oh, I have ways, my sweet. Granted, it wasn't easy. And it cost me a little fortune. But it was worth it. After all, what am I going to spend my money on, if I don't spend it on you? Hmm?"

She closed her eyes and prayed to God for strength. "Only Oscar and my parents have this number. And he wouldn't have taken money from you," she said.

Niles laughed with genuine amusement. "Clementine, there are better, more technical ways of acquiring information than trying to shake down a weasly little lawyer who jumps at his own shadow."

Her teeth ground together. "Oscar isn't afraid of you," she said as calmly as she could.

That caused a loud laugh to come back in her ear and she gripped the phone to keep from flinging it across the room.

"Oh, no. That's why he had security haul me out of his office the other day. But, honey pie, I'm not calling about dear old Oscar. I'm calling to see when you're coming home. Back to Houston."

Her pulse picked up to a rapid, *thump, thump*. "How do you know I'm not there now?"

He made a tsking noise with his tongue. "Now, now, sweetie, don't try to fool your ol' husband. You know that I'm smarter than that."

She bit down on her bottom lip as her mind leaped forward and searched for a way to deal with this maniac. "Niles, has something happened to your memory? You haven't been my husband for a long time now. We're divorced, remember?"

"Hell, that's just a piece of paper, sugar. You know you want to come back to me. You're just playing hard to get. That pride of yours is keeping us apart. But you're gonna get over that soon. I'll bet on that."

Her brain keyed in on the word *soon*. It could only mean he was planning something. Trying to keep her voice as light as possible, she asked, "Oh? Why do you say that?"

"Because—" He paused and laughed in an evil way. "I'm finally going to get rid of your problem. You're finally going to be free to love me again. The way I've always wanted you to love me."

She suddenly felt cold. So cold that she began to shiver. "What, uh, what are you talking about now, Niles?"

"Let's not play games anymore, Clementine," he said, his voice going sharp. "You know what I'm talking about. All that time…I knew there was someone else—some man you took to bed with you every night. You were never able to see me for him, right? You've been pining over him for years."

Fear was causing her heart to beat in her throat and she tried to swallow the quivering thickness. "Who?"

The sadistic laugh was back, but it stopped abruptly and then he spat in a heated voice, "That half-breed sheriff! Quito Perez. How could you stoop so low, Clementine? You come from high-bred Houston stock. How could you have ever lain down with such lowlife scum?"

At that moment she wanted to kill Niles and the reaction scared her. She couldn't allow him to bring her down to his level.

Sucking in a deep breath, she tried to calm herself, to think rationally. "How did you find out about Quito?"

"You think I haven't gone through that little box of yours? I found it a couple of months ago while you were out on one of your little tours of duty for the poor. That badge was laughable, Clementine."

"Why do you say that? Quito's been a county sheriff for fifteen years now. He's revered by his peers and the citizens he protects."

"Yeah, well, too bad they couldn't protect him. That little ambush on the highway nearly got him. And next time, it will."

Niles had never ceased to shock her with his evilness, but this time he managed to buckle her knees and she reached out to grab the edge of the kitchen bar to steady herself.

"How did you know about that?" she whispered the question hoarsely. She was certain the news of the shooting hadn't made the Houston news. The only way he could have known was because he'd been involved with it in some way.

"Oh, come on, sweetie, use that pretty little noggin of yours," he drawled in an all-too-pleasant voice. "Who might want the half-breed out of the way?"

Bile rose in her throat and she slapped her hand over her mouth to keep from vomiting right there on the floor.

"You!" she choked out.

"Oh, sugar, sugar." He clucked with disapproval. "I'm disappointed in you for having such thoughts about me. You know me better than that. I'd never be the trigger man. You know that I'm much smarter than that."

Clementine was gripping the phone so tightly her hand was aching and nausea had caused a cold sweat to break out on her face. The kitchen appeared blurry and she blinked her eyes as she tried to think, to absorb what this demonic man was saying to her.

"So...so you—you hired someone to do the shooting for you?"

"Of course. Keeps my hands cleaner that way."

She struggled onto one of the bar stools and closed her eyes as his sickly charming voice coiled through her like a poisonous snake.

"If you didn't shoot Quito, then who did?" she managed to ask.

He laughed lowly as though he found her interest extremely amusing. "Honey, you wouldn't know him even if I told you his name. So there's really no point, is there? Let's just say he's a man who likes to live on the edge. Especially when he gets paid to do so. And I was happy to pay him well. In fact, he's eager to finalize the task I've given him. You see, he'll get a big bonus when the sheriff is finally dead."

Clementine couldn't hold back her emotions any longer and she screamed at him. "What do you want, Niles? Are you calling just to tell me you're an evil murderer?"

"Don't use that tone with me, bitch! You're not in any position to be defiant with me," he spat back at her. "And now that you've asked, I'll tell you. You get yourself back here to Houston and to me and I just might decide to let your sheriff live. You'd like that wouldn't you?"

Her stomach heaved and once again, she pressed her hand tightly to her mouth. Dear God, what was she going to do? she prayed. If she went back to Houston Niles would find her. He didn't want a wife. He wanted a hostage that he could torture and torment and control on his own terms and wishes. Yet she couldn't allow Quito to be hurt again. Or God forbid, killed because of her. She was going to have to go to Quito, tell him everything she knew and hope he could deal with it. As her lover and a lawman.

Gathering herself together as best she could, she asked in a clear, but shaky voice, "All right, Niles, I'll come home, but it will take me a couple of days to get everything taken care of up here." She didn't bother to plead with him to keep his gunman away from Quito. Even if he would make such a promise, he couldn't be trusted. "And then two more to drive home," she added.

"Till the end of the week then," he said bluntly. "And you damn well better be here by then or you'll wish you'd broken your neck to get here."

He abruptly cut the phone connection and Clementine dropped her own phone onto the bar counter as if it were a nasty piece of garbage.

Shock had turned her legs to useless mush and she wobbled shakily as she made her way through the house to the bedroom.

As she hurried toward the closet to jerk down something to wear, she glanced at the four poster with its tumbled covers. Only a few short hours ago she and Quito had made passionate love there and then she'd slept in his arms, knowing he would always protect her.

Now that Niles had reared his ugly head, she realized it was finally time for her to find the courage to step up and face him. If she didn't, her future with Quito would be over.

After a quick shower, she jerked on a pair of blue jeans and a long-sleeved white shirt. After she rolled the cuffs back against her forearms and pulled her hair into a ponytail, she hurried back to the kitchen and her cell phone.

Since she didn't have a directory, she was thankful Quito had given her the number of the sheriff's department plus his own private cell number. She tried it first, but there was no answer. Not even for her to leave a message. When she called the department, a junior officer answered and quickly informed her that Sheriff Perez was out of the office and wasn't expected back for the day.

Clementine groaned loudly. "But I have to talk to him. This is urgent!" she practically yelled at the young man.

"I'm sorry, ma'am. There's been an emergency over on the reservation that Sheriff Perez is helping with. If your problem is that serious, perhaps you'd better talk with Under Sheriff Hastings," he suggested.

Victoria's husband, Jess Hastings, was a very nice man and no doubt extremely professional. But this was entirely too personal to explain to anyone but Quito. But time was precious. She had to talk this out with Quito. They had to decide what to do before her four days were up. And that was only if Niles kept his word and gave her the four days. For all she knew he was already on his way up here. Probably with a hired gunman.

*Oh God, don't let that be so,* she prayed.

"I can't discuss this matter with Under Sheriff Hastings," Clementine finally managed to respond.

"Well, Deputy Redwing is gone with the sheriff. There's not anyone else here, ma'am," the officer tried to reason with her.

"Listen to me carefully. Quito is the only person I can talk to. It's imperative that I see him! Is there any possible way I could see him if I drove over to the reservation?"

"Good Lord, no! I mean, ma'am, that wouldn't be advisable at all. They're in a dangerous situation over there. You couldn't get near the crime scene anyway."

"Crime scene!" Clementine practically shrieked. "Are you saying a crime has already happened this morning?"

"Uh, no, no. At the last information the department received, Sheriff Perez is okay."

Clementine sighed with relief. "But you don't have any idea when he might return?"

"Not at all. It could be soon. Or not until tonight or tomorrow. Hostage situations are unpredictable."

She rubbed her fingers across her brow as she

tried to think. "I understand," she said finally. The last thing she wanted to do was give this poor guy a bad time. It wasn't his fault that Quito wasn't in town. "If he does come in anytime soon, will you give him a message?"

"Sure, Ms.—?"

"Jones," she said quickly. "Just tell him that Clementine needs to talk to him."

"Got it. I promise I'll give it to him, pronto."

"Thank you," she replied, then quickly hung up the phone and redialed Quito's number. There was still no answer, only ringing, and she could only suppose that he'd turned the instrument off so it wouldn't be a distraction. Or he might have even left the phone in a vehicle.

Sobbing with frustration, she grabbed her purse, tossed the phone inside and hurried out of the house. There was no way she could simply sit here and wait for Quito to return. She had to find him! She had to let him know that her ex-husband was out to kill him.

## Chapter Eleven

Inside her car, Clementine dug a road atlas from under the seat and flipped to New Mexico. She wasn't sure that she remembered how to get to Shiprock or the distance from here to there. Quickly she saw that a good divided highway would take her directly to the reservation town. And with it only forty-three miles away, she could be there in less than an hour.

Once she reached the entrance to the Jones House, she carefully locked the gates behind her just in case Quito should return before she did. The locked gates would, at least, tell him she wasn't in the house.

As she sped onto the county road and headed in

the direction of the highway, another numbing thought struck her.

Did Niles know about the Jones house? She couldn't remember if she'd ever mentioned the place to him. There was a possibility she might have brought it up in casual conversation. But that would have been years ago. She had not had a casual conversation with Niles in ages. Still, she realized from this minute on that she had to behave as if he did know about her former home.

The fear and horror of what Niles had done and was still threatening to do refused to leave her mind even for one second as she drove far above the speed limit through the desert toward Shiprock.

The fact that she'd caused Quito such pain made her physically ill. And if he should have died from his wounds, she would have never forgiven herself. Even if she hadn't pulled the trigger, it was her fault that Niles had hatched such a plan.

Clementine was so overcome with emotion and turmoil that by the time she reached the headquarters of the Navajo tribal police, her arms were limp and she was forced to sit behind the wheel and breath deeply to regain enough strength to get out of the car.

She'd just climbed to the ground when she heard two vehicles coming to a quick halt behind her parked car. Quickly turning her head, she looked through the boiling red dust and saw Quito and two other men climbing out. One of them appeared to be Quito's chief deputy, Daniel Redwing, the other, she assumed must be Yuma Spottedhorse.

As Clementine waited for the three men to gather and head toward the building, she told herself to remain calm and strong. But her nerves had been stretched to such a thin point that tears began to stream down her cheeks.

"Quito!" She took off running in his direction and nearly fell as she stumbled across the loose gravel.

Quito spotted her immediately and ran to meet her. She fell into his arms and sobbed openly.

"Dear God, Clem, what's wrong? What's happened?" He tightened his hold around her and rocked her gently in his arms.

Sucking in a long breath, she said in a muffled voice against his shirt, "It's awful! So awful! Oh, Quito, I know I shouldn't have come here. But I was so afraid."

His hand came up to stroke her hair and pat her back. Over her shoulder, he could see Redwing and Spottedhorse looking on with concern.

"Is there anything we can do?" Redwing asked.

Quito shook his head. "I'll take care of it. You stay here and help Yuma wind everything up. Drive my vehicle home when you're finished," he told his deputy.

Redwing nodded and he and the other officer

walked on toward the police building. By now Clementine had gathered herself together somewhat. She stirred in his arms and lifted her face up toward his.

"I'm so sorry for this."

"Damn it, quit apologizing, Clem. I just want to know what's wrong. Were you scared about my safety? You shouldn't have been. We had several officers with us. And the gunmen surrendered without firing a shot. Everything is okay. I'm okay."

He thought she was worried about this morning. About his work here on the reservation. Oh Lord, how was she going to tell him that it was her fault that he'd nearly been killed?

"Quito, it isn't that. I understand you know what you're doing. It's—" She swallowed and began to wipe at her wet cheeks. "Is there some place we can go to talk? I have something very serious to tell you."

Grim faced, Quito glanced around him. The two of them could go into the police station, but he didn't want anyone to overhear what Clementine might say to him. Especially when he had no idea what this was all about.

"Let's get in your car," he suggested. "We can roll down the windows and catch the breeze."

Once they were settled in to the bucket seats of Clementine's small sports car, Quito turned to her.

"All right. This isn't like you, Clem. I've never seen you fall apart like this over anything. And you look like you've just gone to hell and back. What is it? Has something happened to your parents or some other relative?"

She breathed deeply, closed her eyes, then opened them directly on his face. "I don't know how to tell you this, Quito. But I've found out who tried to kill you. Not exactly who pulled the trigger, but the money man behind it."

He couldn't have looked more shocked and he reached out and grabbed her by her upper arms.

"Clementine! What are you talking about? How could you have found out such a thing?"

She brought her hands up to his wrists and held on to him tightly. "Because this morning I woke up late and I hurried out to the kitchen thinking I'd find you there. Instead the cell phone rang. I thought it was either you or Oscar. But it was the last person I expected to hear on the line. It was Niles!"

Quito frowned as he tried to assemble her words so far. "Your ex-husband?"

She nodded slowly, her expression sick. "Somehow he got my number. I suppose he paid someone to hack into computer information or something. Anyway—"

"Wait! Just wait a minute!" Quito interrupted. "Why would your ex be trying to contact you? Is there something I should know about this man that you haven't told me?"

Trembling now, she covered her face with both hands and tried to keep her sobs at bay. "Oh, Quito, I should have told all of this to you sooner. But I hadn't planned on staying in Aztec. I hadn't planned on seeing you again, on us being together again. I thought you wouldn't want anything to do with me. And then when we did make love, I was terrified because I knew my feelings hadn't changed for you, but I also understood that I couldn't stay in Aztec because it would eventually put you in danger."

His dark eyes were narrowed as he searched her bent head and tried to follow her story. "What are you talking about, putting me in danger?"

Dropping her hands, she looked at him squarely. "Niles is crazy, Quito. He became that way while we were married. He was insanely jealous and had my every move followed. Later, no matter what I did or how good a wife I tried to be, it wasn't good enough for him. The verbal abuse became worse and worse until finally he didn't stop with just words."

Bending his head toward her, Quito slid his hands up to her shoulders and gripped them tightly. "Are you saying that he hit you?"

Shame-faced, she nodded slowly. "It started out with simple slaps. But by then I had totally withdrawn from him and that only made him angrier. Eventually he beat me up pretty badly. I had to be hospitalized and my parents found out about the whole incident." She sputtered, "How could they not when my eyes were black and practically swollen shut? I could hardly tell them that I ran into a door twice. That's when I had to acknowledge that my marriage was a failure and I had to end it for my own safety."

"Oh, God, Clementine! Why? Why did you put up with such abuse? Did you love him that much?" he asked incredulously.

Wide-eyed, she stared at him. "Quito, you don't understand. I didn't love Niles at all."

Quito's head shook back and forth in dismay. "You married him."

She nodded guiltily. "Yes. I tried to pretend that I loved him. Marrying Niles seemed like the perfect thing to do. He seemed to really care about me and I knew he could provide the sort of life I was used to. I was so young and silly," she said in a choked voice. "I was too dumb to realize it was too late for any sort of happy life with Niles or any other man."

"Why?" he asked hoarsely.

"Because my heart already belonged to you. The more I tried to forget, the more deeply embedded you became. After a while I realized that what you and I had together was not something I could easily re-place. In fact, I had to accept the fact that I would never know that sort of love again."

"Oh, Clem. Clem," he said, his voice hoarse with

regret. "Don't keep blaming yourself for all this mess-up. I had something to do with it, too." He pulled her upper body into his arms and pressed her head into the curve of his neck. "When you left I should have gone after you. I should have made you see that your place was with me. But I was full of damned pride. I didn't want to have to admit to myself or anyone else that the only way I could have you was to beg."

Lifting her head, she looked at him through teary eyes. "If you'd come to Houston after me, I would have followed you anywhere," she admitted sorrowfully. "But that's all in the past. All I want now is for you to be safe. And you won't be unless Niles is caught and put away."

"You're saying your ex is the one who tried to have me killed? How do you know this?"

"The idiot confessed to me! That's how! In his grandiose mind he thinks it's something to brag about. He says with you out of the way I can come back to him!" She shivered with revulsion. "Oh, Quito, I'm so scared. I can't go back to Houston! But he says if I don't get back there in four days time, that he'll kill you!"

"Like hell!" Quito growled. "The bastard isn't going to kill anyone. And I swear, he's never, ever going to lay another finger on you!"

Clementine gathered strength from Quito's hard,

resolute voice and she stroked his cheek with a love that had never died, that continued to grow with each hour of the day.

"I never told him about you, Quito. I thought he didn't know there had ever been anyone special in my life. But I had kept the badge you'd given me, your lock of hair and one of the letters you'd written to me. I had them locked away, but somehow Niles found them. I suppose he'd broken into my house before, while I was gone to Afghanistan. That's when he must have hired the gunman to come after you."

"What a psycho," Quito muttered.

"Yes," Clementine sadly agreed. "For the past three years since our divorce, he's stalked me, threatened me, done everything to try to get me back. I knew that soon he was going to start threatening to kill me and probably would. That's one of the reasons why I'd started working overseas with humanitarian groups. The job was not only good for my self-worth, it kept me safe from Niles."

Cradling her face in his palm, he rubbed the pad of his thumb back and forth across her chin. "Is this why you wouldn't make a solid commitment to me?"

Groaning with regret, she said, "I didn't know what else to do, Quito. I knew if I hung around you for very long Niles would find us. And nobody has to tell me what a Wyatt Earp you are. I knew there would be a big battle between the two of you. I couldn't put your life at risk like that. Not for me."

He looked at her calmly, his dark brown eyes gentle pools for her to lose herself in.

"Every day I wear this badge, I put my life at risk," he said softly and firmly. "If not for you, then every citizen of this county. For you, I'd fight a thousand Niles, my darling. And we will fight him. And we'll get him, too. Trust me."

Her hands gripped his muscled shoulders. "But how? We don't have proof!"

"Believe me, if I thought there was a trail of proof, I'd call Jess's brother-in-law, Seth Ketchum. He's a Texas Ranger and a damn good one. He'd put the guy where he belongs. But we can't just use your word. We've got to have more," he mused aloud.

"Maybe I should go back to Texas," she said thoughtfully, while chewing worriedly on her bottom lip. "Oscar would help. Together we might put together some pieces. In fact, Oscar knows a good private detective."

"No. Hell no! You're not leaving my sight. Not for any reason!" he said forcefully.

Clementine eased back from his embrace. "Quito, we can't just sit around and wait for him or one of his goons to start shooting!"

"You don't have to tell me that, Clem. But you've frankly blown my mind with this whole thing. All this time me and my deputies have been thinking the man who tried to kill me was probably hired from someone around here. Now I suddenly find out that our theory was totally wrong. I've got to think about this whole thing, sweetheart. I can't come up with a plan off the top of my head. Whatever we do, we've got to make sure we do it right."

She couldn't have agreed with him more. "What are you doing now?" she asked as he turned back in the seat and reached for the key in the ignition.

"We're going back to Aztec so I can put my head together with Jess. I'll call him from the Jones House. Maybe he can drive by on his way home. The shape you're in right now, I don't want to drag you into town. You need to rest."

The fact that he was so thoughtful of her feelings made her heart ache with love and she reached out and touched his shoulder. "You won't leave me alone tonight, will you? I'm afraid to stay there by myself now that I know what Niles is up to. But I'm afraid for you, too. Maybe we should go to your place?" she suggested with desperation.

He cast her a grim glance as he put the car into gear and quickly wheeled it around toward the adjacent street. "You're not staying anywhere without me. And we're not going to my place. The man might be crazy, but he's clever. Be assured that he knows where my home is. Along with the Jones House."

"But I—I don't think I ever told him about the Jones House," she said. "Especially after my parents willed it to me. By that time Niles had revealed his true character and I didn't want him knowing anything about my financial affairs. Since he was rich anyway, he didn't need my money. And I certainly didn't want him snooping around any of my assets."

Beneath the brim of his Stetson, Quito's brows formed a grim black line. "Darling, you'd be surprised how methodical some criminals are. Trust me, Niles knows about your assets, your bank accounts and everything else that goes down on paper or into a computer data bank."

The idea knotted her stomach and she looked at him with fierce determination. "He's already confessed to me once, Quito. Maybe that's our way to solving this."

Not bothering to look at her, he asked, "What do you mean by that?"

"I'll meet with him. I'll get him to confess again. Only this time I'll have on a wire."

"Hell, no! And don't mention it again," Quito spat. "I'll not have you put yourself in that sort of danger. Not for me. Not for anybody!"

## Chapter Twelve

On the long drive home, Clementine didn't mention her plan again and once they arrived home, she was too drained to say much at all.

She lay down on the couch and, in the kitchen, Quito pulled a wine cooler from the refrigerator and poured it into a tall glass.

When he returned to the living room, he thrust the glass down at her. "Drink this. You need something to calm you."

"I am calm," she protested, but she took the drink from him anyway. "Thanks."

"Drink it all," he ordered. "I'm going to get on the phone and contact Jess."

While she rested and they waited for the under sheriff to arrive, Quito prepared sandwiches and a pot of coffee.

He'd just set the plate of food on the kitchen bar, when Jess arrived and knocked at the door.

From her place on the couch, Clementine could hear the murmur of the two men talking in the foyer. Quito was obviously giving Jess a quick rundown of the situation before he entered the living room. Clementine was glad for that. This whole thing was worse than humiliating. Her past association with Niles made her feel like a criminal herself. It was bad enough just to know that Quito's friend and right-hand man knew her ex-husband was a would-be killer. She certainly didn't want to hear Quito telling him the whole sordid story.

The two men eventually walked into the living room. Clementine started to rise from the couch to greet Jess, but he quickly waved her back down.

"No need to get up, Ms. Jones," he said as he removed a black cowboy hat from his head. "Quito and I are like brothers."

"Call me Clementine, please," she told the tall, sandy-haired man. This was the second time she had met Victoria's husband and she could easily see why her friend appeared so happy and in love. "And I'm thankful to you for your help."

"How about some coffee, Jess?" Quito asked him. "I just made it and some sandwiches."

"I'll take coffee, but nothing to eat. I just finished lunch. But you two go ahead."

Quito gestured to Jess to take a seat. "I'll be back in a minute," he told the two of them.

While Quito went after the drinks, Jess sank into one of the overstuffed armchairs which was squared at an angle to the couch.

Clementine sat on the edge of the cushion and looked at the other man with great concern. "I'm really scared about this, Jess. My ex-husband, Niles, is, well, I actually think he's gone insane. Or maybe he was this evil all along and I just didn't know it. Either way, he can't be trusted to stay put in Houston. Now that he knows where I am, I wouldn't put it past him to come here to try to kill Quito himself!"

Jess held up a palm to hush her voiced fears. "I understand how you must be feeling, Clementine. This whole thing must have been a huge shock to you."

Groaning, she dropped her head in her hand and shook it back and forth. "Niles has stalked and threatened me for a long time now. But I never dreamed he would take this obsession with me to such lengths. Dear God, he's never even met Quito. He doesn't know anything about him, except that I love him."

A few moments of silence passed and then Jess

said, "Most criminals don't have a conscience Clementine. And when a person doesn't have a conscience it's hard to figure what's going on with their thinking. Don't feel badly about this. Just be glad you found out about it in time to do something."

Her head jerked up and she stared helplessly at him. "But what can we do? We don't have any proof against Niles," she miserably pointed out.

"Not yet," Jess said, "but that's coming."

"That's right, honey," Quito said as he entered the room with a tray. "Jess and I aren't Dumb and Dumber. We understand a little about this law stuff. And we've caught one or two criminals in our time."

Clementine rolled her eyes at his joking. "This is serious, Quito!"

"I am being serious." He placed the tray on the coffee table and passed one of the cups to Jess. To Clementine, he handed a small plate with a sandwich and a napkin.

She shook her head. "I can't eat. My stomach is in a knot."

"You can't be of any help if you collapse on us," Quito urged. "Try to eat something. It will make you feel better."

How could he be concerned about her, she wondered, when she'd very nearly gotten him killed?

Quito retrieved his own plate from the coffee table, then sank onto the cushion next to Clementine.

After a bite of sandwich, he began. "All right, Jess, what do you think is the best way to handle this? As far as I'm concerned, I'd like to fly down to Houston right this minute and call the man out."

Clementine stared at him in horror. "You mean like a gun draw in the Wild West? Quito, that's crazy!"

He frowned as he glanced at her. "I didn't say I was going to do it. I said I'd like to. Along with a few other things," he added grimly.

"Well, I think the first thing we need to do is call Seth," Jess replied. "The Rangers can immediately put a tail on the guy. When or if he crosses the Texas line into New Mexico, we'll know it."

Quito nodded. "Yeah. You're probably right about that."

Jess thoughtfully sipped his coffee. "The man's house, offices and car needs to be bugged. I wonder if Seth could pull off a phone tap?"

"We don't have time for that!" Quito exclaimed as he swallowed another hunk of sandwich. "He's only given Clementine four days to get back there. I don't know if warrants could be obtained by then. Or if they could be obtained at all. We don't have any reasons for probable cause. Other than the phone call he made to Clementine. And a judge might view her statement as biased accusations against her ex-husband."

"Biased!" Clementine practically shouted. "The man is the devil incarnate! And I know all about judges. I was lucky to find one who was willing to put a restraining order on Niles on two separate occasions. Neither of which helped one iota. A piece of paper doesn't stop a maniac from coming after you."

Reaching over, Quito took her hand and squeezed it within his. "Clem, you won't have to worry about that ever again," he murmured. "Trust me."

Clementine did trust him to do everything in his power to keep her safe. But that was the whole problem. While protecting her from Niles he would be putting his own life in jeopardy.

She turned her gaze on the under sheriff. "Jess, I've told Quito that I think I should try to get Niles to confess again about hiring someone to kill Quito. And when I do, I'll wear a wire."

Jess studied her thoughtfully, then looked to his boss. "What do you think about this?"

Quito glared at Clementine before he leaned up and placed his plate on the coffee table. "No way. I won't even consider it!"

"But, Quito, it might be our only way," Clementine argued.

His expression was both loving and adamant as he studied the jut of her determined chin and the worried shadows in her eyes.

"I won't let you go to Houston. Nothing you or

anyone can say will make me change my mind about that," he said firmly.

"Maybe she wouldn't have to go to Houston," Jess countered. "Maybe we could get the guy up here on our turf."

Clementine looked optimistically to Quito. "That would work, Quito! You and Jess could be hidden out of sight but close by just in case Niles did try something."

"Could you lure him up here, do you think?" Jess asked her.

Even more hopeful now, she nodded eagerly. "I'm pretty sure of it. I can call his office and leave word that I need to talk to him. Or if I'm lucky, the secretary will give me his private cell number. You two might have some ideas of what I need to say from there on," she said to both men. "But he'll come. Even if I have to goad him into it."

Quito's hand shot up as he quickly rose to his feet.

"Just hold on a minute here. Both of you. I haven't said I would allow any of this!"

"Can you think of a better plan?" Clementine gently challenged.

Cursing under his breath, Quito ran a frustrated hand through his black hair. "Not at the moment. But maybe—with time."

"Look, Quito," Jess said with patient calmness. "We don't have any clue as to who Niles hired to kill you. We can't go that route. It would take too long and we might not ever find out who he is. We have to get that information from Niles himself. He's already told Clementine about his involvement. I'm betting he'll talk more."

"Damn it, Jess, he might hurt her! Can't you understand I can't risk that!" Quito practically bellowed.

Jess did not seem intimidated by Quito's outburst. The under sheriff simply continued to sip his coffee while Quito paced in a small circle around the couch. Clementine could see that Jess had spoken the truth about the two of them being like brothers. Only a man Quito was close to could be as frank with him as Jess was being.

"If we don't put a stop to this somehow, you'd be putting her in more risk of being hurt or even worse, being killed. The man sounds off the wall to me."

"Hell," Quito sputtered. "That's an understatement. I've got scars to prove he's more than off the wall!"

"Quito, what if I asked him to meet me here at this house?" Clementine asked. "That way, you could have total control of the situation. At least, almost total control. There's plenty of rooms and dark spaces to hide in this place. Niles would never know you were around until it was too late."

Quito stopped his pacing and looked at her for long, thoughtful minutes. "You'd be willing to do that? Do you think you could handle it? If you said one wrong word who's to say he wouldn't pull out a knife or gun?"

She sucked in a bracing breath. "I can handle it, Quito. I've been attacked by him before. I'll be ready this time," she said with fierce resolution.

Quito's gaze softened briefly on her face before he turned to Jess. "How quickly do you think we could set it all up? The warrants and all?"

Jess smiled with confidence. "Two days. Give me and Redwing two days and we'll have this place ready to catch a killer."

Quito walked over to Clementine and enveloped her hand between the two of his. His whole demeanor was grave as he looked down at her. "Will you be ready? If not, if you want to back out, tell me now. In fact, I wish you would tell me you've changed your mind. There's other, safer ways to him."

Yeah, she thought, the slow, methodical way. Detectives would begin investigating and gathering evidence and in doing so, tipping Niles off that he was under suspicion and being watched. The man was evil, but that didn't mean his brain was slow to calculate. He'd destroy every shred of evidence involving himself, then play the cool, innocent businessman. Until Niles was taken care of there was no way she and Quito could have a life together. That was the only thing giving her the strength and courage to go on with the plan.

"I'll be ready, darling, to do whatever it takes."

* * *

The next two days passed in a blur for Clementine. The Jones House was infiltrated with lawmen planting bugs in every room and even hiding tiny video cameras in several spots throughout the house.

In her own opinion she believed Quito was going overboard with all the technical equipment, but she also realized his main objective was to keep her safe. And she could hardly scold him for that.

By late evening of the second day, the wires and cameras and tiny microphones were all in place and she and Quito, along with Jess, and Deputy Redwing gathered in the living room. Outside, deputies were stationed in several spots around the rugged terrain of the house and near the entrance of the estate.

Each of the three lawmen were looking at her, waiting for her to finally pick up the phone and dial Niles's number. A few moments earlier, she'd called his office and a secretary had kindly given her his private cell phone number. Now all she had to do was punch in the numbers and pretend she didn't hate the man's guts.

Standing at her side, Quito said, "Don't overdo it on being agreeable to his terms or he might get suspicious. Don't try to hide the fact that you're annoyed with him. Just make it clear you're trying to get back to Houston and you need his help."

At that moment Clementine wanted to simply fall

into Quito's arms and keep her face buried in the middle of his broad chest. But she didn't have that luxury. She had to play this role and play it well.

Nodding slowly, she picked up the telephone. "Okay. I'm ready."

The three men glanced at each other as if to make sure everyone knew there had to be total quietness in the room. Then at Quito's nod, Clementine punched in the numbers and the men picked up the extension phones so they could also hear what was being said.

After three rings, she began to think all the suspenseful buildup to the call would have to be done all over again if the man didn't answer.

But finally the fourth ring was cut short as he connected on the other end.

"Niles Westcott," he clipped out. "Who is this?"

Apparently caller ID hadn't given him the information that she was at the opposite end of the line. Which gave her the slight edge of catching him off guard.

"Niles, it's me. Clementine."

Long, long moments passed without any sort of reply or sound. Clementine looked desperately at Quito and the other two lawmen for help.

But then she heard his soft, arrogant chuckle and realized that he was all too glad to hear her voice.

"So my little dove calls. Been missing me, have you, honey?"

"Not exactly," Clementine answered. "I've been trying to do as you ordered and get on the road to Houston, but I'm having a bit of trouble. I—"

"Don't start it!" he barked the interruption. "There will be no trouble. No delays. Or Quito Perez will see his last sunset. You hear me, bitch?"

From the corner of her eye, she could see Quito flinch at the expletive he'd called her and she knew without being told that he already wanted to kill the man.

"Listen yourself, Niles!" she shot back at him. "If you want me to return to Houston in another two days, then I need your help, not your smart mouth!"

"Well, well. Showing a little spunk for me. I guess that's a good thing. I never did want a puppet for a wife."

"You never wanted a wife. You wanted a slave to do your bidding," she muttered.

He clucked his tongue with disapproval. "Don't get nasty, sweetie. Or you'll wish you hadn't. Now what sort of help do you need? Surely you haven't already gone through the millions your parents left you."

Her jaw snapped together. "Not everyone needs money like you, Niles," she goaded, then said, "I'm having trouble with my car. I have everything packed and loaded, but it's not running right. I've taken it to a mechanic and he says it will take at least a week to get a special part for it."

"That's hardly any trouble. Leave the damn thing there. Buy another one!" he ordered.

She glanced at Quito to see he was shaking his head. To Niles, she said, "Nothing doing. I love that car. I'm not about to part with it. I thought you might fly up here and drive back with me. That way if I have any breakdowns I won't be alone."

Clearly she'd shocked him with the suggestion and Clementine held her breath while praying he didn't find her request suspicious.

"This isn't like you, Clementine. Since when have you wanted my company? Years ago, if ever," he accused.

"Look, Niles, at one time I enjoyed your company. But then your behavior became so abhorrent you gave me no choice but to leave. If you expect us to be man and wife again, then you need to show a little care and concern. The drive back to Houston to gether would give us a chance to talk things over and set some guidelines."

"Guidelines?" he asked, his voice eerily calm. "I'll be setting those. Understand, sweetie?"

Her nostrils flared as she tried to swallow the sickening taste in her mouth. "Only too well, Niles."

"Good. As long as you do, I'll be glad to fly up and

drive back with you. We might even make a mini vacation of the trip. Sort of a celebration of our reunion."

Her hand crept to her throat as the urge to gag
nearly choked her.

"All right," she wearily agreed. "When can I expect you?"

"Tomorrow evening. I have business to attend to
in the morning. But I should be there by dark or
shortly after. Give me directions to where you're
staying."

Relieved, Clementine gave him instructions as to
how to get to the Jones house, then ended the conversation as quickly as she could. By the time she
clicked the end button on the phone, her legs were
weak and her hands were shaking.

Quito led her over to one of the armchairs and
helped her into it.

"You did great, honey. I don't think he suspects
anything."

Clementine's head swung back and forth. "No. He
wouldn't. He thinks I'm too much of a chicken to
stand up to him."

"Well, I think you're damn brave," Deputy Redwing spoke up. "The man is obviously deranged."

"Daniel's right," Jess agreed. "The bastard is not
only dangerous to you and Quito, he's a menace to
society."

Sinking onto the arm of the chair, Quito rubbed

her trembling hand with his. "Are you okay, darling? You're as white as a sheet."

She did her best to smile at him. "I'm much better now that I have the telephone call out of the way. Now if I can just get him to talk when he gets here tomorrow night."

"Don't worry about that," Quito told her. "He sounds like the sort who can't keep his mouth shut."

"Yeah," Jess spoke up. "And you deserve an Oscar for that performance you just gave on the phone. I almost believed you myself."

"Yeah, I did, too," Daniel said to the under sheriff. "But isn't an Emmy better than an Oscar?"

Laughing, Jess grabbed the deputy by the shoulder. "I'll explain it on our way out."

Quito rose to his feet to walk the two lawmen to the door. While the men left the room, she went down the hallway to the bedroom and began to undress.

She was sitting on the edge of the bed, pulling on a pale pink nightgown when Quito entered the room. He came to sit beside her and she sighed with pleasure as he folded her into his embrace.

"This is all nearly over, my darling. And once it is, we're finally going to have the life together that I've always wanted."

She framed his precious face with her hands as she met his gaze. "It's the same life I've wanted, too. I'm just not sure that I deserve it. I'm the one who's caused all this upheaval. And I don't know how you'll ever be able to forgive me."

"Clementine, I don't want to hear any more talk like that. You made mistakes. I made mistakes. Now we're going to right them together. And then we're going to love each other for the rest of our lives," he promised.

Groaning, she angled her lips over his and kissed him passionately. It was the first time she'd really gotten to be this close to him since the night before and the intimate contact set her heart to racing, her nerves sizzling with anticipation.

The kiss was only the first of many and after a few minutes, Quito began to lower her to the mattress. But before he could pin her down, Clementine slipped from his grasp and hurried over to the windows.

As she began to close the Venetian blinds, Quito looked at her with puzzled amusement. "Here you go again with the blinds. What are you doing that for? The light is out. There's curtains on the windows. And we know now that Niles is in Houston, not lurking outside the house."

"Yes. But your deputies are out there somewhere. I don't want them knowing you're in my bedroom."

Rising from the mattress, Quito walked over to where she stood and pulled her body next to his. The corners of his lips tilted with amusement as his fingers played with the blond hair lying against her breast.

"Why do you want to keep that a secret? Is it a sin for me to be in your bedroom?"

Her lips parted with surprise. "Well, no. But I don't want them thinking any less of you. They believe you're a first-class gentleman. I want them to go on thinking that," she insisted.

Chuckles rumbled up from his chest. "And you think they would degrade me for making love to you?"

Her brow puckered faintly as she thought about his question. "You're making me sound silly now," she softly scolded.

Laughing softly, his hands slid to her hips and drew her up against his hard arousal. "My darling Clementine, my men aren't stupid or judgmental. They know how much I love you, how much I want you as my wife and the mother of my children. And they know I'll do anything I have to do to protect you and keep you safe."

She melted against him as her fingers stroked his cheek, then lingered on the faint dent in his chin. "There's nothing more I want in life than to be your wife and give you children," she whispered.

His hands began to knead her buttocks as his lips dipped to the curve of her neck. "I wasn't sure I'd ever hear you say those words," he murmured against her silky skin. "But I was planning on doing everything in my power to keep you here with me." He lifted his head and nuzzled his nose against her cheek. "Do you know what bothers me most about all this?"

She turned her mouth toward his. "No. What?"

"That you didn't tell me about Niles and his abuse. Honey, you must have been living with fear for so long. Why didn't you get in touch with me sooner?"

Groaning with regret, she circled her arms around his neck and held on to him tightly. "Oh, God, Quito, I wish I had. But I didn't want to bring my problems to you. I didn't want to drag you into something that might hurt you. And to be honest, I didn't want you to know how wrong I'd been and what miser-able judgment I'd used in marrying Niles."

"We all misjudge people at times. You didn't ask to be abused," he reasoned in a gentle voice. "And all I've ever wanted to do is love you and protect you."

She sighed with pleasure as his hands pushed the pink gown from her shoulders and slid down her naked body and onto the floor.

"I don't deserve you, Quito. I'm not worthy of your devotion. But as soon as this is all over with we'll get married. And I'm going to spend the rest of my life making it all up to you," she promised. "We'll finally have children and a home together."

"Yes," he murmured as he brought his lips down over hers. "As soon as this is all over."

## Chapter Thirteen

Clementine rose the next morning, determined to keep her nerves calm and steady. She prepared breakfast for Quito and herself, then waved him goodbye as he drove off to work.

Of course, his major work today was making sure everything was set for Niles's arrival this evening. But he and his fellow lawmen had already decided that everything needed to appear normal this morning, just in case Niles had jumped the gun and arrived earlier than expected. So Quito decided to drive in to work just as he normally would, although he'd left behind three deputies guarding the house from areas that even a bloodhound would have trouble nosing out.

Once Quito had left the house, Clementine cleaned the kitchen and straightened the other rooms. After she'd dressed in a pair of white jeans and a red shirt that tied at her waist, brushed her hair and plaited it into a French braid, she went back to the living room to kill time.

Since she had not had time to hook up television service, the only entertainment she had was reading and she spent the remainder of the morning trying to concentrate on a mystery that was far too convoluted for her scattered thoughts.

Eventually she went outside to sit on the porch and while she was there, trying to relax in a lounge chair, she received a phone call from Victoria.

Apparently Jess hadn't leaked any of their plan to his wife. Or he had informed her, but she had the good sense not to mention it over the phone because as they talked, Victoria sounded as though everything was right as rain.

"It's good to hear from you, Victoria," Clementine said. "I've been meaning to stop by your clinic and say hello, but I've been very busy trying to get the house in living order."

"What a job that must have been," Victoria exclaimed. "I'm surprised you didn't come down with dust pneumonia."

Chuckling, Clementine smiled. Thank God her old friend still had the ability to make her laugh and ease her stretched nerves. "I opened all the windows and doors before I started. So you lost a patient," she teased.

"Good. I don't want you for a patient. The reason I'm calling is that I'm having a birthday party for Jess tomorrow night. It's a surprise, so I'm trying to call everyone while I'm at the clinic. We're going to have it over at the T Bar K and Marina, the cook, is preparing a feast. I'd love for you and Quito to come. Do you think you can make it?"

Could they? she wondered desperately. Would the two of them still be together and safe by tomorrow evening? She had to believe so. She had to trust in Quito's ability as a lawman, just as she had to trust in his love.

"Oh, I hope so," she told Victoria. "That sounds so nice. And I remember Marina. Is she still a great cook?"

"Probably better," Victoria said with a laugh. "And having her do the meal means everyone will come."

"Will the rest of your family be there?" Clementine asked. "Your brothers? And your cousin—what was his name?"

"Linc," Clementine supplied. "Yes, he'll be there. That is if we can pry him out of the horse barn long enough to have a meal with his family. And of course Ross will be attending with his wife, Bella. And Maggie and Daniel have already promised that the two of them would show. Unfortunately Seth lives down in Texas, so he won't be able to make it, but we'll still have a houseful with a lot of friends."

"Sounds lovely. I'm already looking forward to it and to seeing your children."

Victoria chuckled. "Hopefully they'll be on their best behavior. And I—" She paused abruptly as another voice sounded in the background. "Uh, sorry, Clementine, I've got a minor emergency here. See you tomorrow night."

The other woman hung up the phone and Clementine pushed the end button on her own phone. Victoria's call had warmed her and for a few moments she'd felt like a normal woman with a family and friends who got together and shared good times.

But now that the call had ended, she looked out at the winding dirt road leading up to the house. How long would it be, she wondered, before Niles appeared. And once he did, would she be able to play her part?

Later that afternoon, Clementine was walking from room to room, trying to keep her mind occupied with plans for refurbishing the house, when she heard the sliding patio doors open at the back of the house.

She had not heard a car or any sort of vehicle arrive. Had Niles parked some distance down the mountain and walked up here for a surprise attack? No. No! He wasn't going to attack her, she desperately tried to assure herself. He was so full of his own ego that he believed with just a little nudge, she would truly fall back into his arms.

Drawing in a bracing breath, she walked soundlessly down the hall toward the living room. Just as she rounded a corner, a male figure was standing right in front of her path. She gasped and jumped back.

Two strong, male hands reached out and grabbed her upper arms. "Clementine! It's me, Quito!"

Nearly collapsing with fright, she shook her head with dismay. "Quito! I didn't hear a vehicle. I thought it might be Niles and I don't have my wire on yet! How did you get here?"

"Don't worry about that now. I just got word from the airport. Niles has landed and he's left in a taxi. Apparently he's on his way."

Sucking in a deep breath, she nodded with steadfast determination. "Okay. Tell me what to do."

Just as he started to speak, a soft knock sounded on the patio doors. She looked over Quito's shoulder to see Jess and Daniel stepping into the living room. The sheriff and his posse were here, she thought, as her insides began to tremble. The shootout couldn't be far away.

"Let's get you wired up first," Quito said.

They joined the other two men and then all four of them went into the kitchen where Quito began to tape the tiny recorder to a spot just above her navel.

"Hurry, Quito. You know how fast Edward drives

that taxi! He'll be here in just a few minutes," Jess urged him.

"Damn it," Quito muttered, his head bent toward Clementine's bared midriff. "I want to make sure the connection is a good one. If we lose their voices then we're up salt creek without a paddle. We'll be forced to go in and blow our cover."

Frowning, Jess paced over to a window that over-looked the front of the house and the long drive wind-ing down the mountain. "If he shows up before we get hidden, our covers will be blown anyway," the under sheriff complained.

"Calm down, Jess," Daniel said. "Quito is almost finished. Besides, think how you'd be feeling if you were doing this to Victoria."

Grimacing, Jess turned back to the little group standing beside the breakfast bar. "Sorry, Quito, I know your guts must be churning now. Let's just get this done."

"Don't worry about my guts," Quito told him. "Clementine is the one who's putting herself on the line." Lifting his head, he looked at her with love and fear and endless admiration. "And all for me."

"Oh, Quito," she whispered fervently. "Don't make me cry now."

His nostrils flared as tumultuous emotions caused him to drag a long, heavy breath into his lungs. Last night as he'd made love to her, he'd kept assuring himself that it wasn't the last time, that he'd have the rest of his life to have her next to his heart. But this evening, as the sun was falling and sending dark shadows over the Jones House, he was feeling more scared than he'd ever felt in his life.

"Just don't do anything foolish," he ordered hoarsely.

Trying to hide the faint quiver in his hands, he smoothed the ends of the tape holding the recorder, then checked the wires one last time before he pulled the bottom of her blouse back over the listening device.

"Am I ready?" she asked.

"Ready." It was all he could say as he looked over at his two deputies with a dark, worried frown. "Are you two ready to get into place?"

Both men nodded and Daniel asked, "Where will you be, Quito?"

"In Clementine's bedroom or somewhere close. I want her to try to lure Niles up to the deck and out in the open. That way we'll have a better shot at grabbing him. He won't have anywhere to run except for a door. And I expect by then for you two to be blocking both doors that lead onto the deck. Got it?" he asked the men.

They both assured Quito that he needn't worry about them doing their job and they left the kitchen to give Quito a moment alone with Clementine.

"I don't know what to say, Clem," he murmured as

he brought his cheek against the side of her hair. "I think by now you know how much you mean to me."

Too full of tears to answer, she wrapped her arms around him and held on tightly until finally Quito was forced to ease out of her embrace.

"I'll be near you. Don't forget."

She nodded, then finally managed to whisper, "Be careful, Quito."

He looked at her one last time, then hurried out of the kitchen.

Clementine looked toward the window to see that night was falling. No doubt Niles would be pulling up any minute.

She'd just walked out to the living room when she heard a car coming up the driveway.

Although she'd been terribly nervous all day, the sound didn't rattle her. In fact, all of a sudden a cool calmness came over her and she lifted her chin and walked onto the porch to meet him.

Niles was a tall, thin man with light brown hair that lapped the back of his collar. He'd always been very vain about his hair and usually had it razor cut every two weeks whether it needed it or not. Tonight he was wearing dark slacks and a pale colored polo shirt. His appearance was immaculate and most any woman who looked at him would think he was an attractive man. But to Clementine he looked like the devil himself.

"Hello, Clem." He dropped the duffel bag he was carrying and stepped toward her.

Clementine's first instinct was to step backward, but she forced herself to keep standing in the same spot as he bent his head and pecked a kiss on her cheek.

"Mmm. You still smell as lovely as ever," he said. "And you look beautiful. This desert air has put roses on your cheeks."

What would he do or say, she wondered, if she informed him that Quito's love had put those roses on her cheeks? Instead she said, "Thank you, Niles. Why don't you bring your bag in and I'll fix us something to drink."

He followed her into the house and all the while Clementine was acutely aware that Quito and his deputies could hear every word being said.

"Nice spread," Niles commented as he tossed his bag onto the couch. "Small, but sufficient. I suppose it would be good for ski trips to Red River. Or we could sell it and buy something closer to Telluride or Aspen."

Clementine stood staring at him and even though she understood he was deranged, it amazed her that he could suddenly just walk in and take over as though nothing had ever happened between them. But then she supposed delusional people were capable of forgetting their sins.

"Sorry, Niles. My parents gave me this home. It

has sentimental value to me. I'm not selling it for any reason."

For a moment his face tightened and she thought he was going to come at her and fiercely point out that he was the boss now. But instead he merely shot her a cocky, all knowing smile.

"Well, we can always discuss it later, sweetie. Right now, let's have that drink. It's dry as hell up here. I feel like I've been eating cotton. Do you have any vodka or bourbon?"

Clementine shook her head. "Beer, wine coolers, or coffee and tea. Or there's milk if your stomach is feeling a bit queasy from the plane ride," she added sweetly.

"Hell, I thought you'd at least have the bar stocked up for me," he said impatiently as he looked toward the small bar in one corner of the room.

"Sorry. We are leaving, remember? There was no point in stocking up the bar," she said stoically.

"Well, like I said, we might be back for a little ski trip."

Over my dead body, Clementine thought as she turned toward the kitchen. "I'll bring you a wine cooler," she told him.

She was pulling the longneck bottle from the refrigerator and wondering where Quito was hidden when she heard light footsteps behind her.

Looking around, she spotted Niles standing directly behind her and she jumped with fright which only made him smile with glee.

"What's the matter, honey? Your nerves a little on edge? I'd hate to think I was the reason for your jumpiness."

I'll bet, Clementine thought nastily. He enjoyed every moment of tormenting, frightening and goading her and they both knew it.

"I'm fine," she lied. "I just didn't hear you."

With her back to the refrigerator, she shut the door and then handed him the chilled bottle. "Here."

He took it and twisted off the cap. Clementine hovered by while he took a long drink.

"Aren't you going to join me?" he asked in a too smooth voice. "A man doesn't like to drink alone, you know."

"All right. I'll have some coffee," she said and carefully stepped around him to the cabinet counter.

After she filled a cup and added a dollop of cream, she turned to him. "There's a nice sundeck upstairs. Why don't we go up there and sit and have our drinks while we talk. There is a fabulous view from there," she suggested carefully.

He shot her a sly look. "What's this? A plan to push me over the railing?"

Forcing her features to remain expressionless, she said, "Believe me, Niles, if I was a killer, I would have already found a way to get rid of you."

His nostrils flared and she could see that she'd angered him. But as Quito had warned her, she couldn't seem too sweet or complying, otherwise, Niles would certainly become suspicious of a trap.

"Well," he said after a long tense moment, "at least you're honest. I suppose it's good to know my wife won't kill me in my sleep."

She walked past him, her chin tilted, her shoulders straight. "Follow me and we'll go up to the deck. It'll be dark soon and we'll miss the sunset."

Just a little longer, Clementine told herself as Niles followed her down the hallway then up the short staircase that led to her bedroom. She hated to take him through that intimate area of the house, but she had the feeling that Quito would be there, close by if she needed him. And since the other way to the deck was a darker, more twisting route, this was the safest course.

"Nice," Niles purred as he cast a glance at the four poster covered with a white comforter. "Maybe we should forget our drinks and stop right here," he suggested.

Her face stony, she glared at him. "Not now, Niles. Before we get to that you're going to have to court me. To assure me you can behave like a gentleman."

He looked at her with immense surprise and then he tilted his head back and laughed loudly. While he expressed his amusement, Clementine hurried out the sliding glass doors and onto the sundeck.

At least she'd escaped for the moment, but she knew before much more time passed, Niles would be pressing her to have sex with him and if she refused he would think nothing of forcing himself on her. There was nothing for her to do but to get him to talking and quickly.

She was standing by the deck railing, pretending to enjoy her coffee when he emerged through the glass doors.

Instead of taking a seat on one of the nearby lounge chairs, he came to stand by her and purposely pressed his shoulder into hers.

The knowledge that she was doing this all for Quito and her future with him stifled her resolve and she gritted her teeth and prepared to stand her ground.

"So how was your flight up here?" she asked in an effort to start a conversation.

"Uneventful. I piloted myself. I didn't necessarily want my pilot to know where I'd gone."

Genuinely surprised, Clementine looked out at the desert hills. "Uh, why is that?"

He chuckled lowly and evilly. "A man likes to keep some things private, Clem."

Maybe he'd come up here planning to kill her, Clementine thought. That could be the only reason she could think of for not wanting his pilot to know of his whereabouts. Or maybe he had plans to murder both her and Quito. Oh, God help her get through this, she prayed.

"You used to be proud of me," she reminded him. "You wanted everyone to know I was your wife."

He sighed. "Yeah. That was when things were perfect. That was before *you* decided to separate us," he said accusingly.

The last of the summer sun was slipping behind the far horizon, casting an orange glow across the desert and purple shadows over the deck. The fast approaching night sent an eerie shiver over Clementine's skin and she was forced to rub away the goose bumps skimming along her arms.

"I've, uh, I've been thinking a lot about that, Niles. I've always tried to be a fair person and maybe you were right about some things. Maybe I just didn't try hard enough to be the sort of wife you wanted."

The words were like chewing nails and swallowing the bits of metal, but she had to get his mind to working and his tongue loosened.

"You're damn right, you didn't try!" he shot back at her. "And we both know why, don't we?"

Clementine did her best to appear innocent. "I tried," she argued. "I just didn't realize how much you cared for me."

He tossed his empty bottle over the railing's edge and Clementine heard the glass shatter on the ground below as he reached and grabbed her by the upper arms.

"So you're finally owning up to your mistakes, are you? This is not what I expected from you, Clem. All this time you've been telling me to leave you alone, to stay away from you. You even had me jailed," he growled.

"That was before I realized that you were only doing all those things because you loved me."

Suddenly the hardness of his features relaxed and he looked at her with an odd tenderness that bordered on insanity. Clementine realized she was walking a very fine line now. If he put his hands around her neck and squeezed, or if he decided to toss her over the edge of the deck, there wouldn't be much she could do about it. He was far stronger than her. She could only hope that Quito reached her in time.

"You're finally speaking the truth," he whispered as he brought his fingers up and began to stroke her face. "You're finally seeing the light. Maybe I will let you live, after all."

She drew in a shaky breath and tried not to pull back in revulsion of his touch. "What about Quito? Are you going to pull your dog off of him?"

"Still worried about your lover? I should have known," he said, his expression changing abruptly to a glare.

"Well, you did admit that you're the one who tried to get him killed."

"So, I did. Why not? The man needs killing. He's

had your heart all these years. All this time that I've loved you and wanted you, you were pining after him." The grip of his hands slipped upward toward her neck. "I should kill you right now for your deceit! And you can bet that I'm not going to let your lover off the hook. My gunman might have failed the first time, but he won't miss this second trip. Your admired sheriff is going to meet his end and you won't be around to weep or carry flowers to his funeral. You'll be with me!"

There was a glazed look in his eyes and Clementine knew he'd entered another zone in his brain where a human's life held little value to him.

"I thought you said you were going to kill me," she reminded him while thinking she might as well get Niles to hang himself on every count.

"I was," he agreed, his voice menacingly sweet.

Clementine felt icy shivers racing down her back as his sleazy gaze slipped over her face, down to her breasts and the juncture of her thighs.

"But I wasn't counting on you looking so good, Clementine. I'd almost forgotten just how gorgeous you really are. Those blue eyes. And the way your long blond hair brushes your breasts. Ah, what a delight your body was."

His fingers curled around her neck and Clementine struggled not to move and fight back in any sort of physical way.

"Now that I think about it, killing you would be a terrible waste. With Perez out of the way, you could be mine. Really mine."

As Niles spoke his warped reasoning, Clementine glanced over his shoulder to see Quito slipping past the glass doors leading onto the deck. Quietly, softly, he crept forward at the same time Niles's fingers were tightening more and more against her windpipe.

"Over my dead body!" she lashed out at Niles. "I'd jump over this railing before I'd let you touch me again!"

Her retaliation was enough to keep Niles's attention occupied on her. He never realized Quito was anywhere near until he grabbed him by the back of the collar and jerked him away from Clementine.

Finally free from Niles grip, she jumped out of the way and stood watching, her hand over her mouth, as Quito spun Niles's around and swung his fist straight into the man's face.

Niles staggered, then fell heavily on his back. Instantly Quito was over him, jerking him up by the front of the shirt and rearing his fist back to hit him again when Niles lowered his head and butted Quito straight in the midsection. The blow was enough to cause Quito to loosen his grip for a fraction of a second and Niles ripped away from him. But one step was all he managed to take before Quito collared him again.

By now Daniel and Jess had rushed onto the deck,

their revolvers drawn, but both of them stood back, allowing their boss to subdue Niles all alone.

Terrified, she glanced hopelessly at Daniel. "For God's sake, help him!" she cried. "Why are you just standing there?"

Keeping his gaze on the two struggling men, Daniel hurried over to Clementine. Taking hold of her arm, he pulled her even further back from the fight. "Quito needs to do this on his own, Clementine. I think you understand why."

Deep down she did understand. But at this very moment none of that mattered. She only wanted Quito safe and Niles put away where he would never have the chance to hurt anyone.

"Daniel! They're headed for the railing!" she screamed as Quito and Niles struggled and fought to the opposite side of the deck.

Jess and Daniel glanced at each other then with a nod of agreement started over to the fray. But before the two men could offer any sort of assistance, Quito once again knocked Niles to the floor of the deck.

Crazed and out of control, Niles bounced up and with a bellow he lowered his head and tried to ram Quito again. Only this time Quito quickly stepped to one side.

Instead of striking the sheriff, Niles crashed into the railing. Beneath his weight, the wood splintered like toothpicks and Niles went flying over the edge.

Clementine screamed as Quito reached out to save the man. But it was too late to make a grab for anything.

Exhausted and grim faced, Quito turned to the three of them and quickly motioned to his partners. "Go check it out," he ordered.

Both men rushed off the deck to do his bidding and Clementine began to sob with relief as Quito walked slowly over to her and enfolded her in his arms.

"Oh, Quito! Quito! I was so scared. I thought you were going to be killed!"

"Shh. Shh. It's all right now, darling," he said between gasps for air. "It's all over with."

Quito decided the best thing to do was let her cry for a few moments to get the emotional upheaval out of her system. He stroked her hair and murmured his love for her while her body trembled against his and her fingers gripped his shoulders tightly.

Her sobs were beginning to subside when Jess shouted from the ground down below.

"Quito! Look at this!"

Easing Clementine away from the front of his body, he closed his hand around hers. "I'd better go see," he told her.

She nodded solemnly and followed him across the deck. When they carefully looked over the broken railing, both of them were shocked to see Daniel hauling Niles, who was very much alive, out of the swimming pool.

"The guy must have nine lives," Jess shouted up to him. "The momentum of his body must have propelled him off the edge of the roof and into the swimming pool."

As Daniel stood Niles on dry ground and snapped his wrists in a pair of handcuffs, he shook his head and sputtered.

"You're all going to pay for this! I'm going to see that every last one of you is brought to trial! You don't have a thing on me. Nothing!"

"Only your confession on tape," Jess told him as he took him by the shoulder and headed him in the direction of one of the squad cars that had now pulled up in the driveway.

The shocked look on Niles's face was almost comical and was enough to make both Clementine and Quito laugh.

"He'll look even more shocked when he's thrown in the state penitentiary. He'll be the one watching his back every minute of the day and night," Quito told her.

Clementine sighed as relief and happiness swirled around her like golden gossamer. The fear she'd lived with the past years was now over. And her life with Quito was just beginning.

"Thank you, darling," she whispered through happy tears. "Thank you for loving me enough to forgive me."

The smile on his lips was as deep and gentle as the emotion pouring from his heart. Wiping the last of the tears from her cheeks, he said resolutely, "We're getting married in a few days. We're going to have lots of kids and we're going to grow old and gray together."

Her smile was dazzling, a wide glorious display of love for him. "That's exactly what we're going to do, Quito Perez. And I've also been doing a little thinking—"

"Uh-huh," he interrupted teasingly. "Blondes aren't supposed to do any thinking."

Feeling light as a cloud, she playfully pinched his cheek, then rising on tiptoe kissed his lips. He quickly caught her head with the back of his hands and holding her, he continued the kiss until he was certain she'd gotten the message.

"I've been thinking anyway," she went on. "I'm going to have this land cleared, barns built and equipment purchased. And then we're going to buy a herd of good horses."

He looked at her with utter surprise. "Why? What about my place?"

"We'll keep it, too, but remember how you used to talk about having a horse ranch? This patch of land would make a great beginning for one. Don't you think? And since you are the beloved sheriff of San Juan County, you'll need help holding down two jobs."

He chuckled. "Where am I going to find it?"

"Right here, darling."

She kissed him again and in the distance, the squad car carrying Niles to jail disappeared into the quiet night.

"We'd better go," Quito finally told her. "There's a few things we need to finalize on this case tonight."

"Yes, like getting this thing off me!" She raised her shirt and smiled as Quito untaped the wires and removed the recorder. Walking with him out of the house she climbed into his waiting vehicle.

They had traveled half the distance to town, when Jess came over the two-way radio and even Clementine could hear fear and desperation in his voice.

"Quito! Daniel's taking Niles on in to jail for booking. Turn around and head to the T Bar K!"

Frowning, Quito turned a dial on the radio and picked up the mike. "Jess, what's wrong?"

"Fire! The horse barn is on fire and the men are trying to put it out!"

"Has anyone been injured?" Quito quickly questioned.

"I'm not sure. I only know that Linc has been burned pretty badly. An ambulance is on its way to the scene."

"I'll meet you there," Quito assured him and hung up the mike.

"Oh, God," Clementine murmured with concern.

"Linc is Victoria's cousin! I hope he'll be all right. Do you think anyone else has been hurt?"

Quito shook his head. "Don't know. We'll have to see," he said, then with a squall of the brakes, he made an abrupt U-turn in the middle of the road, then pounced on the gas.

As the vehicle sped over the dark highway toward the Ketchum ranch, Quito glanced regretfully over at her. "I know you're tired, Clem. You've been through so much, you must be exhausted. Do you think you can make it to the T Bar K?"

With a reassuring smile, she reached for his hand and squeezed it tightly. "I went from here to Texas and back for you. I'm not about to let you down now."

He didn't make any sort of reply, but beneath the glow of the dashboard, Clementine could see a smile of contentment cross his face.

\* \* \* \* \*

*Don't miss Stella Bagwell's next*
**MEN OF THE WEST** *title,*
*TAMING A DARK HORSE*
*Silhouette Special Edition #1709*
*Available September 2005!*

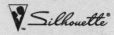

# SPECIAL EDITION™

Go on an emotional journey in

# JOAN ELLIOTT PICKART's

new romance

## HOME AGAIN

**Available September 2005**
**Silhouette Special Edition #1705**

Convinced that her infertility would destroy any relationship, psychologist Cedar Kennedy vowed never to fall in love again. But when dream-come-true Mark Chandler stole her heart and offered her a future, Cedar was torn between the promise of their love…and fear she'll never have a happy home.

*Available at your favorite retail outlet.*

*Where love comes alive™*

If you enjoyed what you just read,
then we've got an offer you can't resist!

# Take 2 bestselling love stories FREE!

# Plus get a FREE surprise gift!

# COMING NEXT MONTH

**SPECIAL EDITION**

### #1705 HOME AGAIN—Joan Elliott Pickart
After a miscarriage left her unable to bear children and her high school sweetheart divorced her, child psychologist Cedar Kennedy vowed never to love again. But when humble construction company owner Mark Chandler brought his orphaned nephew, Joey, in for treatment, Cedar sensed she'd met a man who could rebuild her capacity for love....

### #1706 THE MEASURE OF A MAN—Marie Ferrarella
*Most Likely To...*
Divorced mom Jane Jackson took a job at her alma mater to pay the bills...and now used it to access confidential records seeking information about the anonymous benefactor who'd paid for her education. For help getting to the files, she turned to the school's maintenance man, Smith Parker. Did this sensitive but emotionally scarred man hold the key to her past—and her future?

### #1707 THE TYCOON'S MARRIAGE BID—Allison Leigh
When six-months-pregnant Nikki Day collapsed on her vacation, she awoke with former boss Alexander Reed by her bedside. Alex devoted himself to Nikki's care, even in the face of his estranged father's attempts to take over his business. Their feelings for each other grew—but she was carrying his cousin's baby. And Alex had a secret, too....

### #1708 THE OTHER SIDE OF PARADISE—Laurie Paige
*Seven Devils*
The minute Mary McHale arrived for her wrangler job at a ranch in the Seven Devils Mountains, her boss, Jonah Lanigan, had eyes for her. Then Mary, orphaned at an early age, noticed her own striking resemblance to the Daltons on the neighboring ranch. After discovering her true identity—and true love with Jonah—would she have to choose between the two?

### #1709 TAMING A DARK HORSE—Stella Bagwell
*Men of the West*
After suffering serious burns rescuing his horses from a fire, loner Linc Ketchum needed Nevada Ortiz's help. The sassy home nurse brought Linc back to health and kindled a flame in his heart. But ever since his mother had abandoned him as a child, Linc just couldn't trust a woman. Now Nevada needed to find a cure...for Linc's wounded spirit.

### #1710 UNDERCOVER NANNY—Wendy Warren
As nanny to restaurateur Maxwell Lotorto's four foster kids, sultry Daisy June "D.J." Holden had ulterior motives—she was really a private eye, hired to find out if her boss was the missing heir to a supermarket dynasty. D.J. fell hard for Max's charms—not to mention the unruly kids. But would her secret bring their newfound happiness to an abrupt end?

SSECNM0805